THE TWINS OF NETHERTIME
AND
THE BRIDGE OF TIME

BY
TURNERAMON

Copyright Richard Turneramon 2005

No part of this book may be reproduced, stored in a retrieval system or transmitted by any means without the written permission of the author.

This book is a work of fiction and any similarity to people alive or dead is purely coincidental. No adverse inference should be drawn from places actual or imagined or manners, customs, beliefs or religions, as none is intended.

Cover design by Richard Turneramon.
British Library Cataloguing In Publication Data
A Record of this Publication is available
from the British Library.

ISBN 978-0-9575296-6-3

First Published December 2005
This edition published 2012 by
BonkerBooks
for
Nethertime Publications

www.BonkerBooks.com

NETHERTIME PUBLICATIONS
www.Nethertime.co.uk

DEDICATION

This fairy fantasy is dedicated to the real TWINS OF TIME, *my beloved daughters, Sophie and Laura who show me the way.*

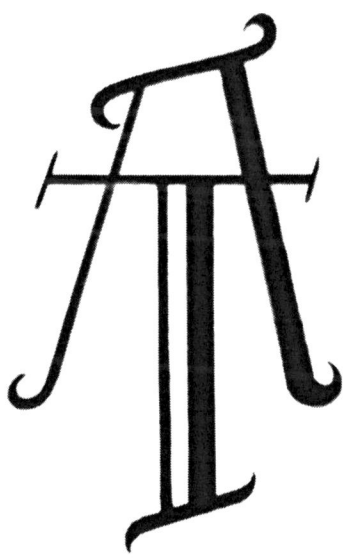

CONTENTS

1. The Bridge of Time 1
2. The Gipsy Kings 15
3. A Highwayman and a Statue 25
4. To rescue the Rhymthus 39
5. The Sunken Kingdom 53
6. At the Shrine of the Oracle 65
7. The Black Angel 77
8. The Etherbeasts 89
9. Troglodytes below 105
10. Flying Lamaphroighs 115
11. The Tower of the Severed Mind 125
12. Saving Maeneid 145
13. Hilderdrake's little game 155
14. The Dungeons of Jahavia 169
15. The Kingdom of Jahavia 179
16. Maeneid's revenge 189
17. The Fairies' Farewell 197

The Bridge of Time

'Let's go, then!' Laura was impatient. She wanted to try out her new bike but her twin sister was taking too long to get ready, for she was insisting on rolling up her black jeans - her excuse being that it looked more "continental."

'That's better.' Sophie put the final touches to her new dress mode, glad that she was out of range of the Sparrow patrol. Sophie was also excited about the new bikes that Sir Marmaduke Merebrook, (or Marmalade as they called their uncle and guardian) had bought them for their eleventh birthdays.

'It's fast!' Laura exclaimed, swerving around in the cobblestone courtyard, 'and the brakes actually work!' She demonstrated this by stopping inches from the massive gates in a cloud of dust, her blonde tresses flying around her excited face.

'C'mon,' she said impatiently. 'Let's go for a spin ... Sparrow will never know and it'll be lunchtime by the time we are back!'

Sparrow was the affectionate name the Twins used for Aunt Asparagus who was not their real aunt but their tutor and nanny. Jailer, more like, you could say, as for years the Twins had been fed up with the strict regime the spindly old spinster had imposed upon them. She hadn't much imagination when it came to understanding the needs of growing children, nor had she a clue as to the outside world; and that was something the Twins were very interested in.

Their incarceration at Merebrook Manor, the home of their Uncle, Sir Marmaduke Merebrook was becoming increasingly wearisome. The Twins, you see, believed themselves to be orphans and had not yet fully understood the fate of their father – but that is another story. And so they yearned for adventure – anything to get them out of the gates of Merebrook Manor. This feeling of isolation was not helped by the increasing number of tourists that came to the historic house after their uncle, in his 'wisdom' had opened it up to the public; thankfully only at weekends for the time being. These visitors only served to illustrate the gulf that separated their cosseted existence from the real world.

'Let's take the needle gate,' Sophie said, and they squeezed themselves and their new bikes through the small wooden door inset into the larger gate. No point in getting Ted, the gardener, to open the big gates; they didn't want to alert any of the staff to the fact that they were bunking off schoolwork. Not that they had any need to worry in that department, for they were bright beyond their years and exceptionally gifted, yet at the same time naïve to the outside world and hence vulnerable.

The Twins rode their new bikes, one green and the other purple, through the extensive grounds of Merebrook Manor, catching a glimpse of the golf course and fairground, recently located on the rolling downs above the distant Torre bay. They exchanged telepathic giggles brought on by the memory of their escapades of last year at the fairground and then they were out of the main gates and free wheeling down the deserted road that led to the hamlet of Merebrook. Then seeing to their right a narrow lane that was unfamiliar to them, they turned into it.

'Strange!' Laura shouted forward to her sister. 'How many times have we been along this road in the Rolls and never noticed this little lane before?'

'Let's see where it goes,' Sophie tossed back her blonde hair, exhilarated with the fresh wind in her face and the bright April sunshine that gleamed from the green spring hedgerows. It was a glorious day.

They cycled down the winding, narrow lane for about a mile, until upon rounding a bend they almost rode into a river!

'Phew!' Laura skidded to a halt inches before the road suddenly stopped. 'Shouldn't that have been signposted or something?'

Sophie joined her and the Twins looked down from the abrupt ending of the tarmac to a slope of grass that led steeply down to sedge grass and then the gleam of blue-grey water as the river glided slowly by.

'It's a bit of an abrupt ending,' Sophie mused, looking at the wooded valley that lay on the far side, its formation seeming odd - like it didn't quite belong to their flatter side.

'Maybe they ran out of tarmac,' Laura quipped.

'Or couldn't afford to build a bridge,' Sophie added.

'What's that?' Laura asked, looking at a piece of tattered paper nailed to a large oak tree at the side of the road.

'Looks like a poster.' Sophie got off her bike to examine it. 'Yep ... it says something about a fête, a fair to be held in Tumbletown ... wherever that is.'

'Tumbletown?' Laura mused. 'Can't be round here ... I'd remember it from the maps.' Both the Twins loved looking at maps and there were many – though mainly old ones – at Merebrook Manor.

'Maybe it's a new town then,' Sophie said, looking again at the poster, 'but there's a bit of a drawing here and if I'm not mistaken it's a sketch-plan and it shows the town's location as right across from the road we're on.'

'Can't be,' Laura joined her sister and screwing up her eyes so that the bridge of her nose wrinkled up, perused the tattered bit of paper that was discoloured and blowing in the breeze.

'You're right,' she said at last, casting her eye back to scan the wooded hillside on the far side of the river, 'but there's nothing there, and no bridge ... odd ...very odd.'

'I know,' Sophie said. 'Let's climb this tree and see if we can get a better view. We might be missing something from down here.'

'Good idea,' Laura agreed, and the Twins set about scaling the large oak tree, which was no mean feat.

Near to the top they rested on a forked branch and surveyed the surrounding countryside. From this vantage point they could see the sweep of the river as it exited the valley and ran into a broad floodplain before reaching an estuary and the sea, which glinted a dark blue in the far distance.

'I can see the lane we cycled along,' Laura scanned the landscape, shading her eyes, 'but I can't see any town...and come to that, any buildings, farm houses and the like.'

'And I can't see the main road either, nor the village of Merebrook…nor Merebrook Manor. Surely, we haven't come that far down the track?' Sophie's voice was puzzled, worried almost.

'Well, it's a mystery.' Laura sighed resignedly. 'We'd just as well go back then. Pity 'cos I would've really liked to have known where this little lane is supposed to lead.'

'What's that?' Sophie was pointing to a slightly lower branch. 'It's a bird's nest, isn't it?'

'Funny bird's nest,' Laura replied, sliding down the oak tree to inspect it, 'it's all lopsided…knocked out of shape, like it was built in a great hurry.'

'And what's that inside it?' Sophie asked.

'I was looking at that. There's some cheap paste jewellery, a lot of feathers and two curious bracelets … but no eggs.' Laura was bending over to reach into it.

'Must be a jackdaw's nest, an old one,' Sophie mused.

'Let's keep the bracelets,' Laura suggested, 'I would like to get them analysed … dated, yer know.'

'Okay,' Sophie agreed, 'it's not really like stealing eggs and maybe someone in the village has lost them. Could be valuable sentimentalia or some such thing.' She didn't really understand the word, but it sounded grand.

The Twins descended the tree carefully, though not without a few scrapes to their knees. They were glad now that they had elected to put on their outdoor gear of black denim jeans and jackets and matching pink and white trainers.

They seemed to be always fighting with Sparrow against the tyranny of a dress code that went out with the ark. And it's not like they were even at school. Because of their questionable legal status and Sir Marmaduke's paranoia about harbouring 'illegals', they were kept locked up at Merebrook Manor most of the time. But they had their own secret and hidden agenda, were conspiratorial in the extreme and kept up with the outside world through illicit television programmes and the Internet. And when it came to subterfuge they could run rings around the spindly spinster 'Aunt' Asparagus.

'Well, I suppose we'll just have to turn around and head back,' Sophie said reluctantly, looking with longing at the intriguing valley on the other side of the river, with its steeply wooded slopes.

'It fits,' Laura announced, having just tried on the oddly designed bracelet. 'Put yours on, 'Ophie ... we can wear them until we get back to Merebrook.'

The Twins sat astride their new bikes, admiring their new finds and looking in growing interest at the intricate modelling on the silver metal of the bracelets that seemed to send out strange messages, catching the light as the sun sparkled from them.

'What are these figures, 'Aura?' Sophie asked, seeming to see dancing, gaily clad maidens come to life, though as she pinched herself the carving resumed its original form: static but intertwining dancing girls ... or were they fairies?

'They are enchanting,' Laura sighed dreamily, scarce able to take her eyes off the fairy-like figures that similarly appeared to be coming to life and dancing around her bracelet.

'I ...I don't seem to be able to take my eyes off them Aura, they are so beautiful' The Twins sometimes spoke to each other in baby talk, particularly when they were confused or upset.

'Come and join us,' the Twins both heard a voice say. But it was unlike any voice they had ever heard before - more like a chorus of the same voice. 'If you like us so much, then why don't you come and join us ... come and join the dance...come to the fête ...'

The magical voices floated off on the breeze and the Twins looked deep into each other's eyes, the sunlight intensifying their bright cornflower-blue orbs so that they appeared fluorescent.

'You heard the voices?' Sophie telepathised to Laura.

'Yes,' Laura responded, 'they were magical.'

The Twins, from a very early age, had been able to share each other's thoughts and silently talk to each other; they were telepathic. But their special gifts did not stop there. For on occasions, normally triggered by mental trauma such as anger, they could move things. At the moment they did not understand where these paranormal abilities came from and treated them with respect that bordered on fear. But they **would** understand them, and more, when the time was right.

'They want us to come and join them, 'Ophie ... they want us to come to the fair.' Laura was looking at her bracelet, seeing the fairy figures flitting around and around in some fantastic fairy-ring dance.

'But I thought fairies only came out at night,' Sophie spoke, looking hypnotically at her own bracelet.

'But it *is* night in our world,' the voices tinkled. There seemed to be several more now, all overlapping; like the same voice but with multiple echoes. And it made the twins feel dizzy, as if their minds were being hijacked by little flitting things, hundreds of them.

'Shall we Ophie?' Laura's voice was distant yet entreating, 'shall we go and join the dance?'

'Why not?' Sophie replied. 'So long as we get back for lunch.'

'For lunch … for lunch … for lunch,' the little echoing voices mimicked, accompanied by a babble of baby laughter that delighted the Twins' ears.

'Okay,' Laura spoke to the invisible voices, clutching the handlebars of her bicycle. 'Show us how … how do we come and join you?'

'Simple.' the fairy voices bubbled. 'Ride over the bridge.'

'What bridge?' the Twins questioned together. 'There is no bridge!'

'You are not thinking hard enough,' the voices replied. 'You have to **think** of a bridge … and **believe**!'

'Think 'Aura,' Sophie urged. '**Think** and **believe**!'

The Twins faced the river astride their bikes, which were

positioned right at the end of the tarmac lane and closed their eyes.

'Think Ophie ... **think of a bridge and believe in it**.'

Gradually the real world started to fade away and the familiar sounds and smells changed - also the light. The bright contrast of sunlight was replaced by a warm, more even, suffused glow.

'Open now,' Sophie telepathised to Laura and the Twins opened their eyes to a wonder of amazement.

'*Incredible*!' Laura whispered, not knowing where to look first, for a huge full moon hung over the hills and the whole visionary landscape was bathed in moonlight. In front of them and joining the lane was a bridge, but unlike any bridge they had ever seen. It hung there in apparent solidity, spanning the river, but its texture was not of brick or stone; it looked like it was made of honeycomb.

In its sides were houses, their windows shining in a lambent flickering of yellow light that spread out onto their narrow balconies and even splotched the grey-green river below with golden reflections.

People were everywhere; small, oddly-dressed people who seemed to be excited, chattering animatedly to one another.

Above these bridge tenements were crenulated walls that again contained dwellings, though these were grander and seemed to be shuttered as though not in use. Across the bridge were hung banners that waved from posts set into the battlements of the bridge. These pennants were decorated with strange motifs of hybrid animals and odd-looking writing.

Beyond the fantasy bridge the Twin's eyes were drawn up to the far hillside. This was steeply wooded as the Twins had observed from the old oak tree, but it now seemed to be populated by a variety of strange-looking buildings that nestled in amongst the towering crystal spires that had magically appeared.

'Welcome to Tumbletown, principal town in the Kingdom of Merrivale.' the fairy voices giggled and the Twins just sat there on their bikes with their mouths open, trying to take in the scene.

'I can see why you call it Tumbletown,' Laura spoke. 'Because a lot of the houses are all higgledy-piggledy.'

'Higgledy-piggledy,' the childlike fairy voices repeated. 'It's all higgledy-piggledy ...'

'Are you ready, 'Aura?' Sophie asked of her Twin. 'Are you ready for the adventure of a lifetime?'

'You bet!' Laura replied jubilantly. 'Let's go for it!'

The Twins, astride their bikes, cautiously edged them to the shimmering join where their world stopped and this fairy fantasia began. The front wheels of their bikes passed over the join quite easily and the girls felt a funny tingling sensation as they passed through the fantasy threshold and onto the bridge.

'Let's ride,' Sophie whispered and the Twins mounted their bikes and rode into unreality. For even though the surface of the bridge felt solid, the hypnotic yellow moon hanging over the tumbled fairy town nestling amongst woods and spires, was surely the most unreal thing they had ever seen.

But to the inhabitants of Tumbletown, it was the Twins who looked unreal. For to their incredulous eyes, the sight of twin giantesses, dressed in some foreign costume of black – a forbidden colour – and long yellow hair, (very dubious); it was as if they themselves were invaded by phantoms. The appearance of these strangers was curious enough, but their shining, fluorescent machines cause consternation amongst some of the fairy folk who just gawped in total disbelief.

The little folk surged onto the bridge, creating a throng of multicoloured, oddly shaped and oddly dressed individuals, who were all babbling at once, pointing to the bikes and their owners.

'Better get off,' Sophie sent to Laura. 'I just hope the natives are friendly.'

The Twins dismounted and stood a bit awkwardly, towering over the chuntering rabble, who, growing bolder by the minute, started feeling the cloth of their jackets and touching the metal of their bicycles. It was quite obvious they had not seen anything like these materials before. Perhaps this was because most of the fairies' diverse clothes seemed to be made of organic materials, like bits of bark sewn together with gossamer thread or leaves stitched with spider grass. On their heads the little people sported a variety of hats made from acorn cups for the men and a more showy display of petals taken from assorted flowers for the women.

'Would you like to ride?' Sophie spoke to the excited

throng that milled around them, thinking it best to start the conversation first. 'Like to ride on my bike?'

'Bike,' the word was repeated around the company as if it was an alien craft, which to them it was.

'Me want to ride *bike!*' a very old man pushed forward, pronouncing the new word as if it were a secret weapon. He lurched unsteadily towards the giant machine, his wrinkled forehead as brown as a berry, his gnarled hands like twigs as they gripped the handlebars.

'That's it,' the Twins encouraged as they unhooked the trailing bottom of his brown tweed tailcoat from the chain, and turning him around, wheeled him back along the empty section of the bridge.

'Me go ... me go,' the grumpy old man rapped the Twin's knuckles with his leathery oaken fingers and they flinched in pain and let him go.

Surprisingly, the crusty old man started to peddle and reached the crest of the bridge without effort. Then gravity took over as he freewheeled down the bridge to where the Twins had entered this strange but exciting world.

'Should we warn him to stop?' Sophie asked. 'You know, where the fairy kingdom ends and reality begins?'

'No,' the voices said. 'Do not warn him ... do not shout to him.'

'Are you still with us?' the Twins whispered.

'Yes, we follow you all the time.'

'So how come we can't see you?'

'Oh you will, when the time is right ... when the time is right.'

'Look!' Sophie said. 'That old man on my bike is approaching the crossover line and he's not slowing ... he's going **straight through it**!'

They all watched the grumpy old fairy, who seemed to be bereft of friends as he approached the end of the fantastic bridge, his tailcoat dragging on the ground. Beyond the imaginary line, the real world could not actually be seen as it was a blur of jangled fog and mists – as if it were not there at all.

Then the wheels of the bike passed over the shimmering join in the fabric of the so-called real and unreal and bike and rider just disappeared. There was not a trace, not even a shadow of them hovering in the swirling moonlit mists; **they were gone**.

The Gipsy Kings

'Who was that old man?' the Twins asked of the voices.

'That was Gorran,' the fairy echoes answered. 'He was our King …the King of Merrivale. But he had become too old, or so he thinks.'

'How old?'

'Four thousand years or so,' the voices replied.

'That's old… even for a King.' Laura mused, nodding her head solemnly.

'Yes.' Came the answer. 'But even if he *is* old he could still be a good King if he chose… if he believed in himself. Only he has let himself become weak and is convinced that he will fall into the hands of the Didicots …'

'**The Didicots**?' the Twins exclaimed together. 'Who in Heaven's name are they?'

'Not in Heaven's name,' the fairy voices were hushed. 'They come from the other side … the bottom side. They are the Ancient Gypsy Kings… and you don't mess with them.'

'So even in such a beautiful place, with people … or beings at least … that live to four thousand years old, there is still trouble, still hatred,' Laura sounded sad, disappointed almost. 'I thought you would all live in perfect harmony … I mean, I know you take children, seize bairns and drag them into your magical kingdom … or at least that is what we read in books …

fairy books.'

'You shouldn't believe everything you read in books,' said the voices. 'But yes, it is true. We do sometimes steal children ... but only those that are fey, they that have the knowing ... like yourselves.'

'So are you saying you stole us from our own world?' Laura's voice was incredulous. 'You tricked us into crossing over the phantom bridge by some Tom Foolery with these bracelets?'

'No we didn't trick you. You came of your own volition, willingly, did you not?'

'You traded on our curiosity.'

'Curiosity killed the cat.' The high-pitched voices laughed.

'We are not cats and we want to go back. And we are not liking the direction this little trip is taking!' The twins spoke firmly as one, their hands on their hips.

'You can't go back,' the voices had stopped giggling and spoke with a more serious tone. 'Not until you have accomplished your mission ... besides, you have yet to come to the fair ... you will enjoy that.'

'Mission?' Sophie was getting a little worried. 'What mission?'

'We are not empowered to tell you,' the voices said. 'We were sent only to bring you through. But you **will** be contacted. Now come and see the fair.'

'Bike, 'Aura ... look, they're stealing your bike!' Sophie had spotted from the corner of her eye a group of suspicious looking creatures whose appearance and dress was very differently from the rest, and who with many a backward, sly glance were wheeling the one remaining bike over the other end of the bridge.

These ruffians were slightly taller and more coarsely featured than their fairy cousins. Their swarthy olive skin was framed by dark curly hair and silver and gold earrings hung from their pendulous earlobes. They wore patchwork frockcoats that draped down to their knees and shiny tight trousers. Like most of the other fairies they went barefoot, except that their feet were enormous and covered in curly black hair.

'**The Gypsy Kings**,' Sophie cautioned Laura, who was striding towards them, intent on getting back her new bike.

Laura either didn't hear or ignored Sophie's warning and she came up to where the group of Didicots stood leering.

'My bike, if you please,' she said firmly.

'Not **your** bike ... **our** bike ... we find it.'

'It is my bike ... I left it here, and I want it back **now**!'

'Or else?' a slightly larger fellow stepped forward. He had the low brow of a pugilist (a street fighter perhaps), and his demeanour, along with his ham-like hairy hands was a bit threatening. Even so, he only came up to Laura's shoulders.

'Or else I will give you a good thrashing,' Laura stood her ground and faced up to the bully.

'**You** will give Rockpile, undefeated champion of one-handed boxing, a thrashing? I think not!' His cronies spoke for him, their swarthy faces leering up at the Twins.

'I think so, unless you give me back my bike!'

'But you are just a *girl*!' Rockpile sneered.

'Well I am eleven!' Laura said proudly. 'And I will give you a thrashing with *no* hands!'

'No hands?' Rockpile turned to his cronies who were holding the bike. '*She* is going to give *me* a thrashing, using no hands!' Rockpile put his great cudgels of hands on his stocky knees and brayed like a donkey in fits of mirth – and his mates did the same.

'You will need a sense of humour,' Laura retorted, standing her ground, 'and let us see if you still have one after I thrash you. Now release my bike or suffer the consequences!'

She took up a stance that was unfamiliar to the Gypsy King and Rockpile's laughter turned to a puzzled frown as he squared up to this alien being, this mortal from another world.

Laura was locked onto him and looking for signals as to a strike or punch. Secretly watching Bruce Lee movies and downloading karate manuals from the internet, she had gone through all the belts in conventional Judo and supplemented a lot of her own style with research from books on the ancient arts of self-defence in the library at Merebrook Manor. All this had been done without the knowledge of Sparrow and though Laura enjoyed martial arts as a discipline, she had seldom had to actually use it and was naturally glad of this.

'Do not fight with the Gypsy King,' the fairy voices warned her at the last minute, causing her to lose concentration and drop her guard.

Rockpile saw this and made his play, opening up with a straight right that caught Laura full on the jaw, knocking her backwards and onto the ground.

'**Laura**!' Sophie shrieked. 'Laura, are you alright?' She knelt down and held her twin sister in her arms. Laura was recovering and feeling her mouth for broken teeth; a trickle of blood ran down her chin.

'Nothing broken,' Laura spoke, pulling herself to her feet, assisted by Sophie. 'Now, Sophie, let me go!'

'Don't go back to fight him,' Sophie pleaded. 'He may be smaller than you but he is ten times stronger!'

'Perhaps,' Laura agreed, her voice becoming steely, 'but he has got me mad, and he has my bike ...*so let me go*!'

Laura pushed away from Sophie, facing up to the ruffian who was doing his little bit of fancy footwork, a smile of victory upon his face.

'Want some more of the same, do we missy?' Rockpile jeered, turning back to laugh at his clan.

'Do not disturb me this time,' Laura spoke into thin air as the bystanders looked around nonplussed, yet seeing no one.

Rockpile was more confident now and more casual. He closed on the mortal and almost lazily delivered a sweeping uppercut, which Laura stepped back from. Then as the missed strike carried the Gypsy King forward, Laura brought her knee up into his groin and then drove her elbow into his swarthy neck and he sagged to the floor. But even before the excruciating pain in his nether regions could register in the fallen Didicot, a side kick followed by a roundhouse kick had him sprawled on the floor not knowing which of his bits to hold first.

'My bike,' Laura stood over him. 'Unless **you** want more of the same!'

'Give 'er the damned machine,' Rockpile gasped, rolling over in agony. 'An' make sure they both gets on it an' rides out of our country, or they'll be 'aving a war on their 'ands.'

'Nasty piece of work,' Sophie sent to Laura, helping her prise her bike from the gawping Gipsy Kings. 'Are you alright?'

'Never felt better,' Laura returned, mounting her bike. 'Now get on the pannier and hold on to me. We are gonna get away from this place before anyone else turns nasty ... and if you hear the voices ... tell 'em to shove it!'

The Twins disentangled themselves from the confusion of little people who were shouting their applause at the spectacle of a Didicot being beaten in a fight, and Laura, with Sophie gripping her tightly around the waist, cycled as fast as she could down the roadway of the bridge towards the swirling mist at the bottom – and the beginning of the real world.

'Hold on!' she shouted back to Sophie, who was trying her best to balance on the rear pannier, her legs outstretched and dragging on the ground. Then came the sounds the Twins were dreading the most: the voices.

'Stop,' they buzzed. 'Stop now ... you will not pass through... it is not your time ...'

'Shut up! We are going back to our own world!' Laura shouted, trying to plug her ear with one hand whilst gripping the handlebar with the other.

'What's happening?' Sophie shouted. 'The bike feels like it's lifting off …'

'I don't know,' Laura replied, looking down to see the front wheel begin to float up from the surface of the bridge. '***It's taking off … I can't control it***!'

The bike lifted off into the moonlit air, banking just before the boundary between the fantasy world and the Twins own world to turn in an arc back across the river.

'It's turning back of its own accord…I can't stop it.' Laura shouted back to her Twin, a note of desperation in her voice as she wrestled with the handlebars.

'And it's sprouted wings!' Sophie shouted forward, seeing a pair of gossamer wings of mother of pearl colours that had magically grown either side of the hi-jacked bike.

'Look!' the people from the bridge below shouted and gesticulated, pointing at the silhouette of the two figures on the winged fairy bike as it flew across the large yellow moon.

'Where are we going, Aura?' Sophie sent telepathically. 'Who's doing this?'

'It's got to be those ones … the ones with the voices,' Laura returned. 'They don't want us to leave!'

The Twins were over the centre of the fantasy bridge now and looking down they could see all the people they had been jostling with a few moments ago. Rockpile, surrounded by his cronies, had picked himself up and was shaking his fist at them. Other fairy folk had stepped out onto their balconies in the walls of the bridge to find out what all the commotion was about, looking skyward in obvious incredulity at the strange airborne machine and its two oversized passengers.

They glided over the river and its bustling bridge towards the steep valley on the far side. This was now in deep indigo shadow, the tall trees that clung to every rock ledge making an opaque barrier through which only an occasional moonbeam could penetrate.

The houses and other dwellings that they had noticed earlier were not so ramshackle looking from here. They were built in odd shapes and at odd angles, perhaps because of the terrain, for the precipitous slopes would surely make it impossible to build normally.

Lazily flapping its new gossamer wings, the self-propelled bike wound around the curving, wooded valley and the tumbled buildings became scarcer, until it was just the tree-lined slopes with their ghostly white spires rising up from the gloom and the glinting ribbon of water below them.

'Look!' Laura pointed, balancing the bike with one hand, 'that building over there looks like a Greek temple!'

Clinging to the steep slope, the strange, ghostly structure was built of white limestone and had a church-like feel to it. Its façade was covered in carvings and an arched doorway with ornately carved columns on either side made it an imposing edifice indeed. Outside was a small terrace on which a large wooden table and several chairs could be seen, though there was no human (or fairy) presence about.

'Hang on!' Laura shouted. 'The bike is turning … I think we are landing.'

The bike came gently down to rest on the small terrace of the temple, the polychromatic fairy wings folding up on their own; it was as if their cycle had been taken over by the fairies or something. The Twins dismounted, leaning their enchanted bike carefully against the wall and stretching their stiff legs and arms.

'Look,' Sophie said, 'there's some grub on that table … lets sit down, I'm famished and parched.'

A Highwayman and a Statue

The Twins sat either side of the large table, rapidly devouring the cold chicken and crumbly bread and quaffing great gulps of what tasted like ginger beer.

'That's better,' Laura belched slightly, loosening her waistband. ''Scuse me!'

They looked up at the temple portico with its jumble of figurative carvings and strange, indecipherable, writing. Then they cast their eyes down over the edge of the stone terrace to the scattering of buildings below that nestled in amongst the white limestone spires gleaming in the indigo gloom. Right at the bottom of the ravine, a yellow glint of reflected moonlight gleamed from the snaking river. One single moonbeam struck the rough- hewn terrace in a spot of yellow as it shone through the grove of tall trees above.

'Isn't this a beautiful spot?' Laura said, feeling somehow more relaxed. 'But it would be nice to know who brought us here, and why.'

'I did,' a deep voice resonated from the shadows. 'But the why of it might take some time to explain.'

The Twins nearly jumped out of their skins. They thought that they had been alone, but now a shadowy figure stood in the arched doorway and he was neither a fairy nor a gypsy ... he was the size of a mortal man.

'Permit me to introduce myself,' the mysterious figure walked into the centre of the terrace, standing near, but not in, the patch of moonlight.

'My name is Gerard Castleton, and it was I who brought you here.'

'We are Sophie and Laura Merebrook of Merebrook Manor,' the Twins rose briefly and nodded, then sat down on the bench to peruse this elegant stranger. He was dressed in a costume they had seen in history books: that of a troubadour. Thigh length riding boots, brown leather breaches and a similar jerkin with much stitching to it were topped by a white lace cravat and a tri-cornered hat. A brace of chased silver pistols were tucked into a broad belt from which hung a cutlass. This swashbuckling effect was enhanced by a cape of green crushed-velvet that hung from his shoulders.

'Are you a musketeer?' Laura asked naively. She had read a bit about such historical characters.

'Good Heavens, no!' Gerard Castleton slapped his leather trousers with a bejewelled hand, his lace cuffs flying in the moonlight. 'Musketeer … what on God's earth led you to that assumption? No, young ladies... nothing as grandiose as that for Gerard Castleton, I'm afraid. Non, no, nope and negative … I am, you see, just a lowly Highwayman, the scourge of the countryside … or so I've been told.'

'*A Highwayman*!' the Twins exclaimed in unison. 'So what on earth are you doing in Fairyland, and what do you want with us … cos you said it was you who brought us here.'

'True, true … and the whole shootin' match of it true,' the dandy struck up a pose, placing one leg on the bench and cupping his slightly bearded chin in his hand he gazed out into the wooded valley. 'Ah,' he sighed, 'the beauty of it all …if only

I had been a painter ... I would have been endowed with fame and wealth ... people would have whispered the name Gerard Castleton in hushed awe, arguing amongst themselves over my works of genius, which was the greatest ... but alas I couldn't paint a pot of pee. Got thrown out of Church School yer see ... and there,' he said, turning dramatically to face the Twins, 'there is the irony of it. It was they, the Church Fathers, who drove me out and set me on the road to ruin.'

'You must have done something a bit more serious than to paint badly,' Sophie observed dryly. 'There are millions of bad painters around and they don't all turn into Highwaymen!' This strutting, self-pitying character was not as menacing as he would like to think he was.

'Well, that is true,' Gerard nodded his head reluctantly. 'I did steal a fair bit of silver plate from the altar, but not the chalice ... I left that for the sacrament ... got to think of others.'

'That was mighty holy of you,' Sophie retorted sarcastically.

'So where is all this treasure that you stole?' Laura asked.

'Ah ha,' Gerard straightened and sweeping his cape in a circle, paced the terrace, his high-heeled riding boots clicking on the weathered rock surface of the terrace. 'It has been stolen.' An expression of abject misery swept across the face of the theatrical Highwayman.

'Stolen?' The Twins didn't know whether to laugh or cry. 'You ... a feared and dangerous Highwayman with your brace of pistols and your cutlass ... and you let somebody steal your treasure?'

'Somebodies,' Gerard corrected.

'What?' the Twins replied brusquely.

'It was somebodies … you know … more than one body.'

'Oh … and who were these somebodies?' the Twins said together. It was obvious Gerard was not going to get much sympathy out of these upstart girls.

'The Fairies.'

'**The Fairies**?'

'Yes … the Fairies stole my treasure. And there was a lot … that is why I brought you here.'

'What, so you can teach us to be highwaymen?'

'No, so you can help me get it back!'

'Help you? How can we possibly help you?'

'Your reputation has preceded you.' Gerard said. 'Your curious powers have been noted by our agents in the world of Mortals. You have been singled out to help in operations… and to get my treasure back.'

'Operations… agent?' The Twins spoke in tandem. 'Are you sure you don't watch too much tele?'

'I know nothing of the so called modern world.' The Highwayman retorted. 'But I did hear about the way you tackled the Didicots and how you beat that blockhead Rockpile … very impressive.'

'You heard about this,' Sophie was making a connection. 'Are you in any way in league with the voices … the ones that lured us into this Kingdom of non-mortals, this fantasy Fairyland?'

'Yes,' Gerard said. 'I am connected to the voices. They are the Rhymthus and they are my friends.'

'And I suppose you can see them?' Sophie asked.

'Yes,' Gerard replied evenly, though he sensed he was being mocked. 'Rhymthus, even as we speak, is perched on your shoulder … but she is very light.'

'Of course.' Sophie looked at each of her shoulders and saw nothing. 'And, I suppose, she can say "Pretty Polly" as well.'

'She can,' the hint of a mischievous smile crossed Gerard's face. 'Do you want her to?'

'I insist,' Sophie wasn't backing down. She didn't believe a word this cockscomb had been saying.

'**Pretty Polly … Pretty Polly**!' a deafening raucous screech of a noise bored into Sophie's ear as she thrashed around trying to knock from her shoulder whatever avian or phantom presence it was that invaded her eardrum.

'Okay …okay,' Sophie held her ringing ear. 'So I believe you. Your friends are called the Rhymthus and one of them is sitting on my shoulder.'

'No,' the voices said. 'You swatted her and she fell off, and then you trod on her …'

'Ohmygod,' Sophie blasphemed. 'I am so sorry … Is she alright?'

'No,' the voices floated sadly on the air, 'we are afraid she is dead!'

'**Dead**?' Sophie looked dreadful. 'How can that be? I didn't mean to hurt her.' The girl was on the verge of tears.

'Only Joking!' the voices laughed and as the melodious sounds fluttered about the moonlit valley, they became visible: tiny, delicate beings, transparent and propelled by scalloped tortoiseshell wings.

'Oh, how beautiful,' the Twins exclaimed together. 'How utterly divine … have you ever seen anything so wonderful … so which of you is Rhymthus?'

'I am … I am … I am,' the fluttering fairies all answered together, their collective voices like the many sounds of nature, lulling, peaceful, yet indefinable.

'How can you all be one … all the same person?'

'They are not persons,' Gerard explained. 'They are emanations… spirits of light. Though they have no individual identity, collectively they stand for all that is good, all that is wholesome. They have no evil in them; they are pure!'

'How absolutely out of this world!,' a tear came into Sophie's eyes as she looked at these spiritual creatures that she had come so near to hurting.

'It would be,' Gerard said heavily. 'Except that the Didicots have captured one.'

'Captured one?' the Twins repeated.

'Yes,' Gerard looked grim, his posturing gone. 'They stole

up on us one evening... Davideous didn't hear them ... they must have been quiet. They netted Rhymthus and took her away to their camp ... all the other Rhymthus are besides themselves with fretting ... they thought a mortal may be able to help.'

'So there is more to our being here than your treasure story.' Laura had it in a nutshell.

'Yes,' Gerard sounded subdued.'

'Well, I'm glad to hear it,' Sophie perked up a bit from her recent trauma occasioned by the mischievous Rhymthus, holding out her hands to touch the delicate creatures who flitted by on the light breeze, their spectral wings catching the moonbeams. 'What do you think, 'Aura?'

'It sounds like a plausible story to me,' Laura answered, 'and if this truly is the purpose for which we were summoned here, then we should do something to help these wonderful creatures of light before we return. It will be a pleasure to get one over on those obnoxious Gypsy Kings, and if that leads to the return of this fine Highwayman's treasure, well then, that's a bonus.'

'So what special powers do you have?' Sophie asked of Gerard. 'Apart from those stuck in your belt?'

'Ah well,' Gerard looked a bit crestfallen. 'These pistolettes don't actually work ... I just wear them for effect ... But we should discuss any strategy as to releasing Rhymthus, with Davideous.'

'Ah, Davideous,' Sophie remembered, 'the one that was a little hard of hearing on the night of the attack?'

'Please don't mock him,' Gerard's face toughened and his hands went down to his brace of silvery pistols; the ones that didn't work.

'Honour among thieves,' Sophie quipped. 'Okay, let us talk to Davideous.'

'Come, follow me,' Gerard walked towards the arched door of the temple-come-church, and the Twins followed, the Rhymthus flitting about their heads with messages of: "thank you ... thank you, oh mortals".

They descended a flight of steps and a vast darkened nave stretched before them. This aisle led down to an altar but unlike any the Twins had ever seen. For where the low altar should stand and reached by four steps, towered a gigantic white marble statue.

Slanted beams of moonlight angled down from giant windows behind, splashing the colossus with stripes of yellow moonlight. The face of the statue, lost in the murk above seemed to gaze down at them, half angel, half devil.

'But this ... this is a famous statue ... surely you didn't steal this ... I mean, it's impossibly big ... how could you do it?'

'I grew it,' Gerard said simply. 'I planted a tiny seed taken from the Vatican, and with patience, and a lot of encouragement, it grew. Beautiful, isn't he?'

'Yes,' Sophie agreed, looking up at the towering statue, 'but isn't this like stealing art, I mean, it's Michelangelo's David, isn't it?'

'*No*!' It was the *statue* that spoke. And in ringing tones that reverberated up and down the dark church-like Temple, setting the bells high above chiming, Davideous continued : 'No, I am not a statue ... I am a living sculpture ... a **person** ... tell them, Gerard!'

As the echoes of the resonating voice and chiming bells faded away, the Twins looked nervously from the colossus and down to the mortal below.

'Yes,' Gerard said dolefully. 'I am afraid it is true. Davideous is actually not a statue ... he is really the blind boy who modelled for Michelangelo's magnificent sculpture of David, the goat herder who slew Goliath as told in the Holy Bible.'

'We know the story,' the Twins nodded their heads. 'So how, why ..?'

'How is he like this? It is all to do with a woman,' Gerard cleared his throat. 'You see, this woman saw the youth modelling for the great artist and she fell in love with him. She was much older than the boy and her unnatural interest was frowned upon by the locals. But she could not help herself, so driven by love was she; so she consulted with an Oracle.

'The Oracle told her to take a cutting of the boy's hair and plant it in a large planting pot. This she did and waited patiently as a small tree grew. She watched and waited throughout the years for the tree to produce fruit and many years later the tree blossomed with catkins. Doing as the Oracle had bid, the woman, who was old now, planted the catkin seed and waited for her beloved David to rise up out of the ground.

'But the Oracle had played a terrible trick on the woman and instead of the youth arising in the spring of his life, a colossal white marble statue grew. The old woman was found one morning at the feet of the statue, her arms round his legs ... she was dead ...she died, it was said, from a broken heart.'

'What a heart-rending story,' Laura said after a while, wiping a tear from her cheek.

'But how is it that the boy lives on in this statue?' Sophie wasn't quite buying it.

'Of all the catkin seeds that grew from that tree, all but one were collected by the Church, who destroyed them. For you see, the story had got around Rome and there was a scandal. The poor woman whom had died of love sickness was buried in an unmarked grave away from her family's vaults.' Gerard sounded sad.

'So what happened to the one remaining seed?' Sophie persisted.

'It was bought and sold by various merchants throughout the years, but no one dared plant it, fearing the wrath of the church, the inquisition yer know.' Gerard coughed.

'So how did it come into your possession?' The Twins asked, not too sure if they were believing this far-fetched story.

'From a blind beggar at Lourdes,' Gerard replied. 'He wanted to take the waters and needed money to buy a candle ... I couldn't refuse him.'

'Well,' Sophie said at last, casting her eye up and down the colossal statue, 'you've had about as much success in getting poor young David out of his statue as you've had hanging on to your treasure.'

'You're right,' Gerard sat on the steps, his back to Davideous, his head cradled in his hands. 'I know not how to release Davideous, even though I would dearly like to help him.'

'Perhaps there is a way.' Sophie said. 'We need to speak to an Oracle … is there such a thing in this, this … place?'

'This **place** is the Kingdom of Merrivale,' Gerard replied pompously, 'and yes, we do have an Oracle, even if he lives a few leagues hence … we are not peasants, you know.'

'Good,' Sophie said, trying hard not to smirk at the self important fellow, 'but all this will have to wait … for we have more pressing business, and it is not the recovery of your treasure, but the rescue of Rhymthus.'

'You are right,' Gerard said, looking up at Davideous.

'*Go*!' the statue boomed. 'Go and bring back Rhymthus … my own release can wait *… I have waited centuries enough*!'

'I will get ready,' Gerard said.

'No,' Sophie retorted, 'you would slow us too much. We will go the way we came…on the bicycle. That is if the very mysterious personage who controls it is willing. We will arrive by surprise … the Rhymthus will guide us.'

'Very well,' Gerard sat down again. 'I will stay here and talk to Davideous … but if you do hear any news about my treasure …'

'You will be the first to know,' Sophie replied sarcastically.

'One thing I want to ask you,' Laura looked puzzled. 'It is not Davideous who guides the machines is it ... our bikes that can fly? And it is not the Rhymthus, is it?'

'No,' Gerard admitted.

'So who is it?'

'It is Maeneid, the female essence of water.'

'Well, that's alright then,' Laura replied, 'so long as she is female.'

'Good luck!' Davideous boomed, unable to help his volume of sound on account of his extraordinary size. 'Thank you for listening to my story. I look forward to our next meeting ... hopefully with the missing Rhymthus.'

'We thank you for your thoughts of kindness,' the Twins spoke as one, looking up at the magnificent Davideous and then addressing Gerard: 'So Maeneid ... does she have other powers ... is she contactable?' they asked of the dubious Highwayman as they sat astride their bike, poised on the edge of the dark blue precipice.

'I do not know of her powers. She is of a higher entity and I am not able to talk to her ... but *you* can, *you* have the knowing ...'

'The knowing?' the Twins repeated. 'Where have we heard that before?

'I cannot tell you.' Gerard made the sign of the cross; a rather strange benediction for a Highwayman. 'But you will know ... you will know.'

'Follow us.' The Rhymthus whispered. 'We will accompany you from here, the Tabanac Temple, to The Bridge of Time along the Moonshine River.'

With that the Twins launched themselves off the terrace on their winged bike, to glide slowly down into the indigo valley below.

☪

To Rescue the Rhymthus

The magically empowered bike, with the mysterious Maeneid at the helm steered a reciprocal course to the one of the Twin's entry into this strange valley of trees and spires through which little moonlight shone. The gilded Moonshine River meandered below as they wound their way around the curving valley of Wendell Dale, mulling over all they had heard up in Tabernac Temple.

Suddenly, they flew into the realm of moonlight, the change as abrupt as from night to day. The large orb of the full moon hung stationary over the hillside as if all time itself was stopped, or put on hold.

All along this journey, the Rhymthus accompanied the Twins, flitting in and out of shade and moonbeams and whispering words of encouragement.

Their visibility, with their slender transparent bodies and gossamer wings of tortoiseshell that fluoresced when they flew through the scattered beams of moonlight had given the Twins confidence. Now they spoke words of wisdom.

'We will disappear now,' their collective voices stated. 'We will be with you, but invisible. We cannot risk being captured by the Gypsy Kings … even one us lost is painful. But we will always be at your side. We will be your eyes and ears. Just listen to us … we will warn you of danger.'

'Thank you.' the Twins said in unison. 'We will return with your kindred spirit, your missing Rhymthus.'

'Courage,' Sophie, on the pannier at the rear of the bike, hugged Laura. 'We will overcome these little Gypsy Kings and find the missing Rhymthus.'

'They are not so little,' Laura replied, remembering the force of the near knock-out punch from Rockpile.

The Bridge of Time was below them and familiar faces looked up at them; a few of the fairy folk waving. Behind the fantasy bridge lay the camp of the Gypsy Kings, a random collection of gaudily painted caravans surrounded by the detritus of everyday living: old broken caravan wheels, discarded horse halters and bridles, rooted and flowering sacks of old potatoes, etc. etc.

'Let's land before we get spotted,' Sophie sent, and the Twins were lowered down to land gently on the long grass by a copse of wizened old beech trees.

'Thank you, Maeneid,' the Twins looked up into the moonlit sky, but saw no one.

'She says "Welcome",' the voices replied on her behalf.

'Stash the bike,' Laura muttered, covering it with an assortment of rotten branches and long grass. 'Now,' she said, cracking her fingers back in an ominous sort of way, 'let's go and parley!'

The Twins headed for the Didicots' campsite, not too sure what they would find, but with a feeling of anticipation.

'Psst!' a voice came from the nearest caravan. They looked and saw a woman's face at one of the small bull's-eye windows that was open a crack.

'Psst! Come over …come in …'

The Twins skirted round the end of the caravan, treading quietly, not too sure what sort of introduction to expect from this stranger.

'Come in …come in,' the woman was peering nervously from the upper section of the stable door of the caravan, beckoning the Twins to enter. They did so cautiously, looking around the dark interior as the woman quickly closed and bolted both doors and drew the heavy brocade curtains so that only a narrow strip of moonlight illuminated the interior.

"Ave ye come ter take me boys away?' the woman asked anxiously. She collapsed heavily on one of the cushioned seats, gesturing for the Twins to sit opposite. Her face of indeterminate age seemed heavily made up although it was difficult to make her out as she sat in the shadows.

'Tell me yer not 'ere ta take me boys!' The woman gasped.

'We …' Sophie, taken aback, was about to answer.

'Yer see,' the woman interrupted, breathing heavily, 'they're not bad boys … not really. A bit rough and ready behind the ears …but they're not bad boys … not like Hilderdrake …'

'Who?' the Twins spoke as one.

'You know, Hilderdrake, the conqueror of Merrivale, the one great commander this lackadaisical world 'as 'ad.'

'We don't know about that,' the Twins looked at each other – there was more to this Fairy realm of Merrivale than met the eye.

'Anyway up,' the middle aged lady relaxed visibly in her chair, 'so yer not after me boys ... ah's very, very gladdened in me heart to hear that ... let me introduce meself. Me name's Mandrake ... Mrs. Sivelus Mandrake, ter be precise ...pleased to meetcha!'

'The honour is all ours,' the Twins rose from the comfortable seats and bowed briefly.

'Such manners.' Mrs.Mandrake nodded. 'Ah jest wish me boys could meet up wid girls like you. Ah mean, when yer were a bit older, that is ...'

'Naturally,' the Twins nodded, still preferring to keep this strange introduction on a formal level.

'So, iffin yer don't mind me askin',' Mrs. Mandrake asked, leaning forward so that the sliver of yellow moonlight touched her face, giving her an appearance of a block of granite, except for the remnants of a tear on her solid cheekbone, 'so why *are* yer 'ere?'

Telepathic signals flashed between the Twin's brains as they wrestled with choices. Firstly, the guilt they would feel at telling this anxious mother of Rockpile - for that is who they guessed she was - that they were here for him. Secondly, the desire to be truthful. The latter won out.

'We want to talk to Rockpile,' Laura said in measured tones. 'We think he may be able to help us release the Rhymthus, the being of light that we hear is held captive in your camp.'

This explanation could not have had a more dramatic effect than if you had lit a stick of dynamite under the Gypsy Queen's chair. Mrs.Mandrake jumped up vertically from it, crashing her dyed black mass of hair on the wooden framed ceiling.

'Rhymthus ...Rhymthus, did yer say? Ah will not 'ave that kind of talk in this 'ouse! Dae yer understand? Ah will not 'ave the curse 'o the Lamaphroighs visited upon this 'ouse ... dae yer catch me meaning?'

'No,' Laura stood up, a steely set to her eyes. 'No, Mrs.Mandrake, I do not understand! The Rhymthus are not your enemies. They are beings of light ... defenceless. As for the Lamaphroighs, I am sorry, but I have never heard of them!'

'The Lamaphroighs are mercenaries!' Mrs. Mandrake spat. 'Paid soldiers! They came 'ere with Hilderdrake to ransack and pillage this Kingdom of Merrivale. Now the Gypsy Kings and Queens are a proud clan ... our family tree can be traced back thousands of years. So when the Lamaphroighs invaded our people centuries ago, we fought and lost. Some of our offspring are Lamaphroighs, but we are not of their ilk, we are **human** people, trying to eke out a human life. We are not of them ... not of their hybrid wasp-like unnaturalness.'

Mrs. Mandrake's voice had been dragged down into the depths of depression as she recounted the story of her ancestors defeat at the hands of the Lamaphroighs back in the distant past. The Twins could not help sympathise with her and they leaned forward and patted her hand.

'We're so sorry,' the Twins consoled. 'We didn't realise your history. That would explain the character of Rockpile ... he is a throwback ...'

'Throwback 'e may be,' Mrs.Mandrake dried her eyes. 'But 'e is me favourite son ... and I love 'im!'

'Of course, of course,' Laura was starting to feel a little sympathetic to this strange woman. 'And we have to be careful not to get into any more fisticuffs. But if you could tell us where we could find the missing Rhymthus, then we could be gone from here with her, and no one would know ...'

'Iffen ah tell ye,' Mrs.Mandrake leaned forward, her breath smelling of alcohol and tobacco, whilst a shaft of moonlight splashed across her ample bosom, causing the milk-white of her skin to stand out from the rich red satin of her voluminous dress, 'Iffen ah tell ye ... then ye must keep it ah secret ... between you an' me, do ye agree?'

'Okay,' the Twins nodded, relieved when the Gypsy Queen sat back in her chair. Her physical presence was a bit disconcerting to say the least.

'Now then, the reason they captured yon fairy in the first place was so they could win the fishin' match.'

'Fishing match?'

'That's right ... they wanted to catch a biggun, a steelypike ... six footer or so,' Mrs.Mandrake held out her arms as far as they would go. An', of course, as lads do, they thought ter throw a bit o' luck their own way ... so they used the little bundle o' light as bait ...'

'**As bait**?' The Twins were sounding even more disbelieving. 'What kind of outrage is this?'

'Well, ah knows it's not the done thing,' Mrs.Mandrake said. 'But them lads needed ter win a bit o' money. They was owin' on the rent, yer see. So anyway up, they bags the biggest steelypike yer ever clapped eyes on!'

'But what about the poor Rhymthus?' Laura shouted.

'Well, that's the point, yer see. They was about ter gaff it, an' it ... well, it slipped the 'ook.'

'You mean it got away?'

'Fraid so.'

'With Rhymthus still in its jaws?'

'Worse.'

'The steelypike ate the Rhymthus?'

'Fraid so.'

Laura stood up, her head scraping the ceiling of the caravan. As anger, shock, disgust, sorrow and a whole gamut of emotions raged through her mind, a nimbus of silver-blue light played around her head, crackling like the static energy from some dysfunctional transformer.

'By the Altar-God of the Great Jahavia,' Mrs. Mandrake blasphemed. 'Yer, me child, 'ave the power ... an' yer 'ave the knowing ... now ye'll not go 'armin' me boys, will yer?'

'No, Mrs.Mandrake,' Laura had control of her fit of rage, 'we give you our promise ...we will not harm your boys, but we need to enter into a bargain with them. If we help them to re-catch the steelypike, then they give us the Rhymthus.'

'They'll be as 'appy as Larry to do that,' Mrs.Mandrake brightened. 'There is still the prize money waiting, for whoever catches that whopper and they will be as pleased as Punch, so they will.'

'Goodbye,' Mrs.Mandrake waved a hesitant wave, as the Twins walked down the steps from the caravan. 'An' may the Saints of the Travellers protect ye ... ye'll find Rockpile down by the river, under the bridge.'

'How on earth are we going to find a fish in these miles of river?' Sophie asked, glad to be away from that dreadful woman and the smelly caravan.

'Maeneid find fish,' the voices spoke.

'Of course,' Laura cheered up. 'Maeneid is a water spirit ... she can show us where that steelypike is. I just hope that Rhymthus is still alive inside it.'

'So let's walk down to the bridge and confront Rockpile,' Sophie said. 'The bike should be alright where we hid it.'

The Twins walked away from the caravan camp of the Gypsy Kings and down the meadow towards the river that wound its way lazily under the great buttresses of the busy bridge and through the fields of gold.

Under the massive arch of the bridge that spanned from the near bank to the middle of the river, were a group of anglers. They were encamped around a fire and seemed to be paying little attention to their rods, which were laid out in a haphazard fashion, a variety of coloured floats bobbing in the dark waters.

'Well, well, what 'ave we 'ere?' the unmistakable profile of Rockpile rose from the card game he had been playing with his cronies.

'We come in peace,' Laura spoke quietly, yet firmly. 'We

come to trade.'

'Trade is it now? Well, ah don't tink you 'ave anytink that ah want, young missy,'

Rockpile was about to sit down again but Laura spoke: 'Wouldn't you like a chance at the steelypike again?'

'An' 'ow would yer propose doin' that?' Rockpile asked suspiciously.

'I will deliver him to you here,' Laura sounded more convinced than she actually was, 'and in return I ask you not to harm him before he releases Rhymthus.'

'Ah!' a streak of sadistic understanding flashed in the Didicot's. 'So it's the little people yer after 'elping now? … Well, that's more *your* kind o' game.'

'Is it a deal?' Laura pressed the lout, who stood there leering, his mop of black hair hanging down onto the long, draped, patchwork frockcoat.

'A deal it is, little missy … you deliver the same steelypike here to my rod. I will knock 'im on the 'ead with me club an' you can take little fairy frolickins, an' ah will keep steelypike an' claim me money … couldn't be better.'

'Right,' Laura said. 'Stand by with your rod and your club, because here he comes,' then talking to fresh air: 'Rhymthus, are you in touch with Maeneid? Has she found the steelypike?'

'She has.' the voices replied. 'Look up river, you will see him. He is out of the water some of the time. He is being directed against his will and is angry … and he is a big one!'

'Look!' Laura pointed under the arch to the river upstream. What looked like a wave - or more like a tidal bore - was approaching at speed, a menacing dorsal fin breaking the surface of the placid moonlit waters.

'By the Saints!' Rockpile oathed. 'Tis the one an the same as I 'ooked t'other day ... ready, me lads, ready with the clubs an' the gaffs.'

'You're not going to gaff it,' Laura cried. 'Are you forgetting who's inside?'

'No,' Rockpile leered. 'No, we're not forgettin'.'

'Does Maeneid hear this?' Laura asked of the invisible Rhymthus.

'Yes. But she says not to worry ... she has an idea.'

The Twins directed their attention back to the river. It seemed as if the whole population of the bridge had seen this massive freshwater fish steaming along at a rate of knots. People craned over their balconies above to catch sight of the phenomenon, taking bets on whether Rockpile would be able to re-hook it or not.

As it approached the shadowy depths under the arch, a row of small, but ferocious looking teeth could be seen just under the water, set in the form of a malevolent grin. Then the fish stopped swimming, and to the amazement of the onlookers raised its head out of the water, looking at them with doleful piscine eyes. And then started to belch!

First one loud belch could be heard, and then another that echoed around the arch of the bridge and which brought total disbelief to the eyes of the anglers. One final burp and the steelypike opened his razor teeth wide and out flew the Rhymthus, visible in her aura of transparent gossamer and wings of tortoiseshell. She was quickly seized by her other selves, her sister Rhymthus who were now visible, and they flittered under the arch of the bridge with much rejoicing.

'Now,' the repatriated and joyful Rhymthus spoke to the Twins, a note of jubilation in their voices, 'now for the other end of the story ...a very fishy end indeed!'

As the Twins watched in utter amazement, the steelypike, instead of flopping back down into the water, rose onto the bank in a standing position, its broad tail supporting its considerable weight, and lunged at Rockpile. Before the Didicot could move an inch, his head, followed by his body, disappeared into the cavernous mouth of the fish that shook the carcass down its gullet and "walked" backwards into the water.

Not a sound was uttered by those on the bank as they stared in dumb stupidity at the submerging steelypike, a satisfied grin on its face as it sank beneath the black waters.

'Well,' Laura stood with her hands on her hips. 'I promised that I wouldn't do anything to harm Rockpile ... and I didn't.'

'Remind me not to mess with a water spirit,' Sophie said as they walked away from the dumbfounded Didicots, their mouth slack with disbelief.

Soon the news was all over the town and the denizens of the bridge houses were bringing out extra tables onto the balconies. 'Come and join us, come and join the party!' they shouted down to the Twins. 'Come and tell us first hand what happened!'

As you might expect, the Twins were the flavour of the 'day' and were invited from one house party to the next, plied with cakes and ginger beer and persuaded to repeat their story yet again; the jubilation of Tumbletown was beyond belief.

The Twins partied on most of the night, but as there was no time in Tumbletown (the full yellow moon remaining fixed over the towering crags) the concept of night didn't really mean anything.

'Well,' one old codger said, yawning and tapping out his clay pipe, but carefully, 'I'd better be getting me 'ead down ... moon'll be up soon.'

'Moon'll be up soon?' the revellers mocked him, swigging their ginger beer. 'Moon's been up for fifty thousand years ... or 'adn't yer noticed?'

'No,' the elderly fairy retorted, 'but by the raggedy looks on your faces, ye surely 'ave.'

'Git ye ter yer measly bed,' the grumpy friend replied. 'You're not the stuff o' parties. ... So tell us one last time, young missy, 'ow came Rockpile ter a fishy end?'

The Twins gave their account one last time, sitting on the balcony of the bridge house tenements and looking out onto the winding Moonshine River.

'Ah 'ate ter think what 'is poor mother'll do,' an elderly woman said, looking sadly into her empty glass. 'Rockpile was 'er favourite boy ... an' she 'as a few connections ... the Lamaphroighs fer a start.'

'The Lamaphroighs don't frighten me. They is jest the cannon fodder of the Ancient Ones what controlled this Kingdom thousands o' years ago, the ones what fell from grace.' a younger man spoke, holding onto his young lady as if to steady himself. 'It's Hilderdrake and Mandrake what worries me ... ah mean, they two was lovers once ... thousands o' years ago.'

'What, Mrs.Mandrake was Hilderdrake's ... you know?' the Twins looked stunned.

'Mrs. Mandrake is it now,' the youth spat over the balcony into the indigo river below. "Er as is called Sivelus ... well she be a lot more 'un she seems. She made pretend ter be a Gypsy Queen an' says she 'ates the Lamaphroighs, but 'er other self knows 'er true nature. Cos she be a regrown Ancient Queen. Queen o' the Lamaphroighs!'

'Regrown?' Sophie enquired. 'Do you mean resurrected?'

'Ah don't understand yer fancy words, young missy,' the young man said dismissively. 'But ah do know this ... she is older than time itself ... an' she 'as got some pretty nasty tricks up 'er sleeve. She is, ter tell God's 'onest truth, *a witch!*'

'**Witch**!' the gathering on the balcony drew back from the speaker as if they themselves might catch some witchery from his very words.

'A witch she is!' The man retorted. 'An' I 'ears as she is a practitioner 'o black magic an' more asides!'

Well, we had best be going,' Sophie was beginning to realise that these little people were not as harmless as they appeared to be and that their welcome was not all inclusive.

The Twins made their farewells, sorry to leave the festivities but glad to turn their backs on the recent conversation. For at the mention of the word "witch" the mood of the partygoers had changed to become more sullen and even menacing.

The Sunken Kingdom

The Twins walked back to their bike, and hidden by the copse of wizened old beech trees, were careful to avoid being seen from the caravan camp, especially by Mrs.Mandrake, the so-called ancient witch.

They found the bike intact under the brushwood and mounted it, speaking to the Rhymthus. 'Are you there? Are you with us? Can you ask Maeneid to fly us please?'

'We are with you,' came the reply, 'and Maeneid has asked if you would come to her abode. She would like to talk.'

'Yes, of course,' the Twins replied. 'But we don't know where she lives.'

'She will guide you to her, she will fly you.'

'Of course,' the Twins replied sheepishly – it was a bit obvious, wasn't it?

Once more, with the Twins astride it, the bike was magically lifted up into the air and they flew over the Bridge of Time. The revellers had mainly gone inside to sleep it off, but a few die-hards raised their glasses as the Twins flew overhead. Then they retraced their journey along the Moonshine River as it wound through Wendell Dale, flying past Tabanac Temple. They looked up to the terrace but it was empty. Gerard had gone to bed, they supposed, whilst Davideous presumably was as silent as a statue.

The bike was headed towards a fork in the river where a

great megalith of eroded limestone towered up from the wooded spur of the ravine. This marker of the ways was capped by a turreted tower. At the base of this part natural, part man made structure was a fissure in the rock suggesting an entrance of sorts. Extending outwards from this natural portal lay a small circular terrace that overlooked the confluence of the two rivers. Standing on the terrace in a long scalloped dress of white silk reaching down to her bare feet was a young woman, her tresses of silver hair catching the angled moonlight.

'Maeneid,' the Twins telepathised as their bike descended. The image they had conjured up of her couldn't have been more accurate.

'Welcome,' the beautiful young woman held out her hands as the Twins landed on the terrace and propping their bike against a rock, walked up to her.

'We can hear you,' they said.

'I'm sorry,' Maeneid replied. 'I had to be careful. I have kept this home of mine and my presence here a secret for so long ... I had to be sure you were not spies.'

'Spies?' the Twins looked astounded.

'Yes,' the water spirit looked sad. 'Even in this beautiful place there are those who would harm us. But come,' she said, brightening and taking their hands, 'let me show you my domain.'

Maeneid led the Twins back across the terrace to the small entrance; the fissure at the base of the towering sentinel of rock that dominated this beautiful, yet forbidding valley.

Ducking their heads to stoop below the low arch that dripped ice-cold water onto their necks, the Twins were led down numerous winding steps. They could hear the sound of splashing waves and smell a fresh sea breeze that wafted up from below. Rounding a bend they saw a vast ocean stretching before them that faded into the misty distance. Either side the rocks rose upwards until they disappeared into the void above. The whole vast panorama was illuminated by a turquoise light, suffused yet constant, and a little way out to sea the silhouette of a tropical island could be discerned.

'This is my retreat,' Maeneid murmured, 'my world within a world.'

'It is so beautiful,' the Twins could scarce get their breath at the shock of this unexpected watery world within a cavern, let alone offer any logical or geological explanation as to its existence; they were, after all, in "Fairyland".

'My barge awaits us,' Maeneid gestured down to a narrow quay that was built into the sandy cove, fluorescent green waves lapping over it. Besides this jetty was moored a giant shell that bobbed up and down in the shallow sea and to which were attached four monstrous turtles. They embarked, stepping gingerly onto the fan-shaped scallop and on a command from their mistress, the turtles started to swim, towing the water spirit's 'ferry' towards the island whilst Maeneid told the Twins something of the history of the Kingdom of Merrivale.

'It was once a happy place,' Maeneid explained. 'Remote, cut off from the world of humans and the various clans of fairies, gnomes, goblins and kindly folk lived out their long lives in peace and harmony. Then Merrivale was invaded from the north by Hilderdrake, Mandrake and the Lamaphroighs, a devilish mixture of resurrected sub-humans and wasp-men. They didn't break through the time perimeter, but came in by way of the Sea of End World and the Caves of Thorg …from the sea and underground.

'They enslaved the local people, who put up little resistance, but after some thousands of years they grew bored and returned to their own country of Lamaphroigh, to the north. But they left a few, like Sivelus the Mandrake, who thinks she is a Gypsy Queen, thanks to a spell put on her by Hilderdrake who sought to ditch her for a younger woman. Let us hope her memory of her former life is not reawakened, for she has residual powers to reanimate the ancient ones, the Mytho-creatures.

'What do you mean?' The Twins asked, a frisson of revulsion tingling up and down their spine.'

'I didn't mean to frighten you.' Maeneid said, looking in concern at the ghastly faces of the strangers. 'And let us hope you learn nothing of such things, but all is not as it seems in what you call fairyland.' The water spirit shivered to her spine, took a deep breath and continued.

'Rockpile was a Lamaphroigh, but thanks to you and myself he is well taken care of … fish food that is. Yet there are others like him who wish the gentle people harm … that is why I was cautious and checked you out first.'

'What of Davideous and his curious friend Gerard Castleton, the Highwayman?' Laura asked, looking in awe at the willowy maiden who sat cross- legged in the "bow" of the shell, her silvery hair blown about her face by the sea breeze.

'Highwayman!' Maeneid laughed. 'Is that what he is calling himself these days? Beggar or cutpurse more like. Yes, he and his trusty statue Davideous are something of an enigma.'

'Their story sounded convincing,' Laura said.

'Convincing sounding, yes ... but I wonder ... I wonder.' Maeneid stood up, a hint of a frown crossing her brow.

'These turtles are far too slow,' she said, almost petulantly. 'I will give us a bit more speed.'

She unhitched the turtles and raised her arms, her long white sleeves blowing in the breeze and the Twins stared over the side of the giant shell in amazement as they saw it lift off and rise from the sea.

At the same time there was a jolt and they were flung backwards into the ribbed cup of the scallop and felt the rush of acceleration.

'Hold on!' said Maeneid. 'Oh, sorry! Am I a little too late?' The Twins were not sure if she was finding their fall amusing or not.

'This is the way to travel!' Maeneid shouted over her shoulder, standing legs astride in the prow, her silver hair streaming out behind her as the shell skimmed over the bright, jade-coloured waves, spray flying up either side.

'Look!' Sophie exclaimed, pointing beyond the bow of the shell. 'Flying fish!' And to be sure a school of flying fish had joined in the mad chase, breaking surface and then gliding on long transparent fins to follow the telekinetic hovercraft of the distant past.

'My island,' Maeneid said proudly, slowing down the

speeding shell. 'Let me show you the ruins of Atlantis.'

'**Atlantis**?' the Twins repeated stupefied. When was this never-ending adventure going to stabilise into normality?

'Look!' Sophie pointed to the island, a frown of incomprehension puckering her perfect brow, for there was something very curious about it.

'It can't be,' Laura stared in disbelief. 'It's floating … whoever heard of a floating island?'

'I keep it in hypersuspension,' Maeneid said. 'It's more difficult for the Sholags to climb up onto it if it's off the ground … sea, that is.'

'Sholags?' the Twins queried, looking up at the natural rock buttresses that formed the walls of the strange island.

'Sholags … sort of barrels of lard with tentacles, they do make a mess.'

'Octopus!' the Twins exclaimed.

'Similar, only with one hundred tentacles, not eight.'

'Are they dangerous?' Laura asked.

'Well, they do have a partiality to medium-sized, blonde-haired girls,' Maeneid laughed, a high, infectious musical laugh.

Using her superior powers of telekinesis, the water spirit held the shell hovering in front of a natural rock arch, whose giant buttresses were reminiscent of Notre Dame, or some other great Baroque cathedral.

Then Maeneid, controlling the giant shell with her kinetic mind drew them slowly through the massive portal to land on a flat plinth of grey-green rock.

'Step carefully,' she said, 'this level is a bit slippery with seaweed.'

They followed her across the seaweed-covered plinth of rock to some stone- cut stairs that led up to a golden bridge attached to a golden pagoda. 'To see my sunken Kingdom we have to take the lift.'

'The lift?' the Twins exclaimed. Their only experience of a lift, apart from when one of them had got stuck in one, was the dumb waiter in Merebrook Manor. Heaven knows they had played long enough in that, much to the annoyance of Cook and Asparagus – or 'Cock-sparrow' as they had called the hapless pair – for they could never catch them as the Twins had sussed out all the secret passages of Merebrook Manor by the time they could crawl.

'Climb aboard the gondola, the bathysphere or whatever else you want to call it.' Maeneid was gesturing at a strange-looking contraption that was housed in the golden pagoda. It was made of brass and copper and a profusion of tubes of some rubbery material wound themselves around it in an elaborate tangle.

'Air on,' Maeneid pulled a massive lever and there was a hiss of a compression mechanism. 'And release!' She smiled as she threw a great handle located on the floor of the contraption and the Twins felt a jolt as the antiquated capsule, suspended by a thick cable, moved slowly out of the pagoda and down towards a central hole in the "floor" of the floating island. As it submerged into the sea and slowly descended, the colours seen through the portholes changed from light jade to an increasingly deeper shade of aquamarine,

'I find this a very relaxing way to descend,' Maeneid remarked, smoothing her silken hair back from her face. 'Like this you can enjoy the visual delights of all the treasures that this sunken continent has to offer, even though I could swim down more quickly.'

'Did you discover this yourself?' Sophie asked. 'Atlantis, that is.'

'Heavens no, child ... Atlantis sank millennia ago and though existing in legend, no one quite knew where it was located. It was the Atlanteans themselves who revealed its precise location. They were being threatened by Hilderdrake, Mandrake and the Lamaphroighs. But they, like us, are a peace-loving people and had no stomach to fight, so we sealed them in this time cavern and here they have remained unmolested for millennia.'

'You mean they still live in Atlantis?' Sophie asked. 'I mean, how do they breathe all this way down?'

'Oh, they have developed gills and are quite happy on land or water ... there look, they are welcoming us.'

The Twins looked out from the bathysphere and saw a sunken continent, resplendent in its former glory. Porticoes, arches and windows were cut out of the coral that now encapsulated the fallen temples and ancient pylons that stood as an enduring testament to a lost world. Gaily coloured fish of all varieties and sizes swam in and out of the columned temples and coral arches, illuminated by the fluorescence from above.

Then the Twins saw a group of people gathered under one of the massive pylons; they were waving.

'I will go and say hello now … you stay here,' Maeneid said and the Twins turned to look at her and gasped. The white gossamer dress had gone and in its stead gleamed rows of tiny scales. Her beautiful face was disfigured by a pair of long gills that grew either side of her still recognisable face. Where her slender legs should have been was a tail, curled and forked.

'You've turned into a mermaid!' Laura blurted.

'Well, I *am* a Water Spirit.' Maeneid replied, and with that she was gone, walking backwards awkwardly, as the steelypike had done, into the submersion compartment to exit outside the bathysphere and swam rapidly towards the waiting Atlanteans.

'Did you see the way she flipped her tail?' Laura exclaimed. 'It's just like the dolphin stroke that I've been trying to do.'

'You'll have to get her to teach you when she gets back,' Sophie said dryly.

Soon Maeneid returned, accompanied by a throng of mermen and mermaids who swam around the gondola, waving and gesturing. Their scaly skin was a mottled golden-green as shafts of light penetrated the azure depths and their golden hair floated around their youthful faces.

Maeneid said her final farewells to the Atlanteans and re-entered the bathysphere, dripping seawater onto the floor as she changed back into her 'mortal' shape. She pulled a lever and the underwater capsule headed slowly up towards the surface.

'Thank you for showing us the lost Kingdom of Atlantis,' the Twins took one last look at the fading Kingdom. 'We will treasure the memory.'

'That's one thing the Lamaphroighs didn't find,' Maeneid mused, 'the treasure.'

'There is treasure down in that ruin?' Laura gawped at the fish-woman, although it made perfect sense.

'Treasure beyond belief.' Maeneid whispered. 'Stored by the Phoenicians, before the island sank and now guarded by their mutant offspring, the Atlanteans.'

'Still, no one can get to it, can they?'

'Only spirits of water,' said Maeneid.

'But they are all good, aren't they?'

'There are a few, a very few, who are evil …'

But the bathysphere had docked in its golden pavilion and the three exited, walking back across the bridge and onto the seaweed plinth to where the shell sat on the slimy flat rock.

'Come,' Maeneid said, climbing aboard the shell. 'I must get you back to Tabanac Temple; there to complete your mission … you must go to the Oracle.'

The Twins looked at Maeneid. They were wondering how she could know of their own suggestion as to repatriating Davideous with his body, but her face spoke "no questions" as she projected the giant scallop at a rate of knots towards the distant shore. Soon they were standing on the moonlit plinth under the towering pinnacle and mounted the bike as Maeneid bid them farewell.

At The Shrine Of the Oracle

'So,' Gerard Castleton paced the terrace, 'I congratulate you on your success at freeing the Rhymthus.'

The Twins had flown on their winged bike from the Tower of Maeneid to the Tabanac Temple, accompanied by the chattering Rhymthus.

'Thank you,' the Twins replied, 'Rockpile came to a fishy end.'

'So I hear,' Gerard stopped his pacing and swinging one thigh-booted leg onto the bench, he looked quizzically at the Twins. 'And I also hear that you have seen a few other sights …'

'Well, Maeneid showed us her Lost Kingdom, if that is what you mean,' Sophie retorted, not quite liking the sarcastic tone this poser was taking.

'**Her** Lost Kingdom, is it now?' Gerard spat, vehemence in his tone all too evident. 'And I suppose you didn't enquire about the whereabouts of my stolen treasure?'

'We didn't really have time,' Laura snapped. 'I mean, she took us down to the bottom of the sea in some sort of weird contraption. The only treasure we heard about is the ancient treasure of the Atlanteans.'

'Oh well, that's alright then!' Gerard said sarcastically. 'I suppose that little pile of sunken treasure is far more important than mine.' Although Gerard's voice was sour, a new light seemed to burn in his eyes. 'What about me?' a deep voice reverberated around the interior of the Temple. 'Anybody make any suggestions about helping *me* out of *this* rockpile?'

They walked into the temple and up to the towering marble statue of Davideous.

'The Oracle,' Sophie spoke, looking up at Davideous. 'Maeneid said to further our mission we must go to the Oracle … it is like I was trying to tell you… an Oracle tricked that poor woman who fell in love with you as a youth … and to spite her it was that Oracle who turned you to stone … so it is an Oracle who must revoke the spell and restore you to your human self and size. Now where is the *nearest* one in this peculiar little Kingdom of Merrivale?'

'A long way from here,' Gerard said. 'We must trek up through the Forest of Lum and cross the plain of Rhan, then avoiding the Old Temple of Jahavia we will reach the forum of the Oracle at the base of Scollock Edge. This is a towering escarpment standing next to the Sea of Endworld that marks the boundary of the Kingdom of Merrivale.'

'What, you mean we have to walk?' Sophie interrupted scathingly.

'I'm afraid I don't have one of your contraptions with wheels and wings, and I don't think Maeneid could transport the three of us, even if she was so inclined.'

'Well, let's get going then,' the Twins said together.

'Well, so I will just wait here for your return.' Davideous said glumly.

'We will be back my stony friend...we will return with the cure for your statuesque solitude...your years of silence...your...'

'*C'mon!*' The twins cut through Gerard's rhetoric. 'This no time for poetry, if that is what you call it.'

They set off from Tabernac temple, taking a track that led up through the lower scree slopes, then climbed for an age up a winding path that zigzagged through the Forest of Lum. This wilderness was mainly comprised of larch and blue spruce trees that made the path gloomy, except where relieved here and there by a sprinkling of silvery broad leaf or the occasional dapple of yellow moonlight.

Then suddenly they were at the top and the dazzle of the hypnotic full moon once more blessed their faces. Reaching an overlook, Gerard stopped and breathing heavily, pointed down into the blue-grey distance.

'There lies the Plain of Rhan, and over there the Caves of Thorg to which we must go.' He pointed towards a distant massif that rose out of the swathes of mist. 'We have to get to that knoll just to the right of the Old Temple of Jahavia at the base of Scollock Edge.' He pointed back towards the Plain of Rhan.

Squinting into the far distance the Twins could just make out two features, one glinting with a golden light.

'Well if you ask me,' Sophie said, 'it's out of our way to go via the Caves of Thorg. Why don't we just walk down through the forest and across the plain in a straight line?'

'A straight line?' The failed Highwayman mused, stroking

his weak chin. 'You're right,' he sighed, 'navigation was never my forté.'

They set off from the overlook, walking along the winding path leading down through the Forest of Lum. The terrain gradually changed: the trees became sparser and soon they were walking on soft and springy grass that increased the length of their stride, they were down on the flat unending Plain of Rhan.

The curious trio tramped endlessly through eroded gullies of spongy moorland, whilst avoiding the numerous peat bogs and dead tree stumps hung with trailing Spanish moss and sprouting strangely coloured toadstools and puffballs. At last they topped a rise and saw they were nearing the base of Scollock Edge, though an aching weariness had set in long before. Taking a deep breath, they set out resolutely to cover the remaining distance between them and their objective and after a while reached it.

Before them stood the Forum of the Oracle, its low earth banking forming a circle in which a variety of trees grew. A multitude of birds were busy warbling and cooing, nestling or fighting in the dense branches of the circular arbour.

'This way,' Gerard said, striding through the only opening and into a field of long golden grass. In the centre of this large enclosure stood a craggy hill, itself overgrown with trees and trailing creepers. A natural fissure appeared to be the only entrance.

They squeezed through the rocky cleft into a space open to the sky and saw immediately ahead a pillar upon which stood the carving of a hideous face; the whole overgrown with green creeper so that the eyes stared out fiercely from the darkened depths.

'Behold, The Oracle!' Gerard introduced the effigy, his voice slightly nervous.

'You come from Maeneid,' the Oracle spoke, its stony lips, wedged in a tangled beard, scarcely moving at all. 'What news from Atlantis?'

'It's still rather wet,' Sophie said, smirking slightly.

'Ah, humour … and of the very childish kind … how refreshing. And how is Davideous?'

'Still as a statue,' Laura blurted as Gerard frowned. He wasn't used to talking flippantly to Oracles. He knew what they could do to a man if they were not amused.

'Oh, yes,' the Oracle's voice was level. 'It is the other one of this bright pair of mirrored-minds. I would have thought you could have gone one better, but obviously not … you come for my intervention, do you not?'

'We come to ask you to entreat your comrade in Rome … Sixteenth Century Rome, that is, to help us release the blind boy Davideous.'

'I don't need a history lesson,' the Oracle said. 'I **make** history! What I need to know is why … why is this petrified boy in this strange little Kingdom of Merrivale, as also is this over-dressed dandy?' The Oracle's eyes moved jerkily to scan Gerard. 'And my other question … is he not happy as a statue?'

'Well, he doesn't have your fortitude,' Sophie spoke. 'Unlike you he hates his stony state and as a young man he longs to be free ...'

'Free ... Oh, yes,' the Oracle sighed, 'what sins have been committed in the name of freedom? I cannot remember what it was like to be free ... so many millennia have passed.'

'You mean, you were once human?' the Twins blurted, looking at the aged face, its lines lost in the long hair and beard now covered by a grey-green patina and blackberry-eating birds' droppings, pips and all.

'Oh absolutely!' The Oracle's voice took on a more interested timbre. 'I was once a philosopher, and a good one. I did so well at postulating the hypothetical that instead of being apotheosised I was metamorphosed into an Oracle ... and without my permission, as well.'

'And did they give you a dictionary to go with it?' Laura retorted rudely as Gerard almost blew his top.

'Sarcasm is the lowest form of wit.' The Oracle rebuked.

'So why have you remained in a job that you don't particularly care for, for so long?' Sophie asked.

'Hum, good point,' the Oracle looked confused, perhaps for the first time in his life. 'Probably because all my friends are dead and I am just a relic ... no where else to go ... though people do respect me yer know, particularly when they want to know what the future holds in store for them. But I did prefer being a philosopher... I mean you didn't have to be so dramatic; doom and gloom and all that. Well maybe a little bit of gloom.'

'You could join us,' Laura blurted. 'We'll be your new

friends. Release Davideous as your last great charitable act and then release yourself!'

'What a wonderful idea!' the Oracle's voice had a bit of a break in it. The stone effigy thought for a moment and then nodded, chunks of patina flying off his tangled hair and beard. The multitude of birds in the trees had stopped singing, having detected some supernatural event was about to take place.

'Stand back! I am going to do a double re-invocation ... never been done before. I need to home in on Davideous in the Tabanac Temple ... Yes, yes, I have him ... Hold on!'

As his deep voice died away, the birds in the trees took flight and a deep tremor rumbled up from the ground. The encircling crags shuddered and more patina pinged off the statue.

Suddenly, an arc of silver-green energy gushed up from the pedestal, enveloping the Oracle in a flaming aura. It surged up in a spiralling inferno to rise high into the moonlit night and then arced down far away and out of sight.

'**Resist me not**!' the Oracle's voice reverberated around the fractured crags. 'Jahavia, Melsuik, Calades, resist me not or I will break thy web ... I will destroy our bond!'

In reply to this celestial challenge, multicoloured vectors of supernatural energy arced across the sky, intertwining with the green, as if to strangle it or break its hold. But the Oracle stood his ground and slowly the stone casing around him began to melt, chunks flying off to release a molten magma from beneath that dripped onto the ground.

Finally the task was finished. The combatant energy bolt

dissipated and a more human figure stood where the pedestal had been, blackened, smoking and steaming.

'And now for a bath,' the charred figure said and a geyser of water spurted up from the ground, warm and steaming, enveloping the former Oracle in a fountain of cleansing spray.

'Drying off,' the figure spoke, still dripping so that his face was covered in wet hair and beard. A group of cherubs suddenly appeared in the sky above, blowing down their warming breath so that the emerging mortal looked like he was under a very large, celestial, hair dryer.

'And finally, clothes.' An assortment of raiment floated down from the sky, to land miraculously on the overhanging branches. 'There!' the re-born old man said. 'How do I look?'

'I wish I could get showered, dried and dressed as quickly as that,' Laura said enviously.

The former Oracle emerged from the centre of the glade, his long white hair and beard styled into loose waves, his dark, penetrating eyes full of humour as he scrutinised the three. 'How do you like my choice of wardrobe?' he said, parading the loose pleated toga that swept the ground leaving a pair of golden slippers just visible.

'Welcome to the humble world of humans,' Gerard plucked up courage to speak.

'What do we call you?' Laura asked.

'And do you still have your powers?' Sophie added.

'My name is Socrates,' the seer bowed. 'And before I was

turned into an Oracle my teachings were known throughout the civilised world.'

'They still are,' the Twins whispered their tone reverential. For this was the man of which they had read so much about, actually standing here in the flesh before them.

'How encouraging,' Socrates bowed. 'Now, as to your second question … my powers … let me see.' He pointed a forefinger up to the sky, directing it at the ever-stationary moon. Then he moved his finger quickly and the moon moved too. Quickly he moved it back to its original position, hanging over the ragged rim of Scollock Edge.

'Don't want to fiddle too much with nature, now do I…particularly not in a fantasy setting…might spoil the effect.' Socrates said.

The birds that had returned after the previous rumpus and were trying to get their heads down to have a sleep, took one brief look at this supernatural occurrence, twittered slightly and settled down again…it wasn't that threatening, just showing off really.

Socrates continued. 'Yes, I think I can safely say that my powers are back, though I have lost the ability to see the future. But that is of little import so let us see if my double re-invocation spell has worked. Let us go and gaze once more on the beauty of Davideous!' Socrates set off with an unerring stride down the hill of trembling grass.

After a tortuous hike walking back across the Plain of Rhan and up to the Forest of Lum they descended the pine- covered slopes leading down to the Tabanac Temple. Panting for breath on finally reaching the temple, they saw a slim youth, teetering on the edge of the terrace above the precipice.

'**No, Davideous ... No**!' Gerard rushed towards the blind boy in an attempt to stop the former statue from plunging to his death, but he was too late. Davideous, unfamiliar with the outside of his former prison, had stumbled over the edge.

They looked in horror, as if in slow motion, at the descent of the blind boy from the terrace as he hurtled down to the scree slope of broken rock below. Even as Socrates raised his hands to intervene - though too late now - a shadowy figure, barely visible, snatched the youth up in its arms and returned him to the terrace. And before anyone could draw breath, the black figure flew swiftly away, her lithe form and golden scalloped wings visible for one instant as she flitted through an errant beam of moonlight.

'Davideous,' Gerard seized the boy in his arms, 'you are released from your marble form; you are returned to your own self.'

'And yet you are still blind,' Socrates spoke, 'and I was too slow to prevent your fall.'

'What was that thing that saved me then?' said Davideous. . 'Its body was as cold as ice.'

'I fear that was a black angel,' Socrates sounded sombre.

'**Black Angel**?' the Twins gasped. 'What in Heaven's name are they?'

'Not in Heaven's name, I'm afraid,' Socrates stroked his long white beard. 'They are renegades, fallen angels that were expelled from Heaven millennia ago. Now they wander the world and all its Dimensions, looking for evil employ!'

'So if it is evil, why did it **save** Davideous?' Gerard asked.

'Yes,' Socrates frowned. 'That is a puzzle. It is out of character for a black angel to do good … there must be a deeper reason … like you are meant to be kept alive.'

'As you were meant to resume your mortal self.' Davideous' sightless eyes 'looked' at Socrates.

'Perhaps,' the philosopher replied. 'Perhaps there is something afoot that we are not aware of. But we need to be on our guard. Black Angels are used a lot as spies, as they are almost invisible.'

'Pity we don't have an Oracle to consult any more,' Gerard said resignedly.

The Black Angel

Several 'days' had past since their return to the Tabanac Temple and Davideous' dramatic saving. They had eaten and rested after their recent exertions, but nagging doubts plagued the Twins shared minds, although they said nothing to the others.

'It is good to see the Rhymthus returned to themselves, having been repatriated with their one lost self.' Davideous said, having recovered somewhat from his near death experience, his voice a wonder of childish delight as he "watched" the barely visible creatures flutter in and out of the moonlight.

'How can you see them if you are blind?' the Twins asked.

'They send me pictures,' the young man replied. 'Images of themselves … it is truly delightful.'

'And can you talk to them?'

'Of course!'

'I wonder?' the Twins exchanged telepathic signals.

'What?' Davideous turned his head, not sure if he had heard anything or not.

'Rhymthus,' the Twins spoke softly, 'can you hear us?'

'Yes we can,' the multitude of voices replied.

'Can you tell us ... is there any other being like yourselves with wings, but black. Is there any such a being in this building now?'

'There is,' came the echoing answers.

'Where is she?' the Twins whispered. 'Don't let her know you are looking, but where is the Black Angel?'

'She is up on the roof truss, sitting on the centre of that big beam of wood. She is looking down at you and the boy she saved, Davideous. But she looks sad.'

'Thank you, Rhymthus,' the Twins looked at each other. 'Shall we try?' they sent to each other, for this so called Black Angel was a puzzle, one of the enigmas of this topsy-turvy world that intrigued them above all others.

The Twins of Time locked their minds into a configuration that more than doubled their mental powers. They projected it upwards, creating a visual impression of how the Black Angel sat, lithe legs crossed atop the ceiling beam, although they themselves were looking straight ahead.

'Greetings,' they magnified their telepathic signal, directing it up towards the invisible figure. They heard a slight movement, as if the Black Angel flinched in sudden shock. 'Greetings,' the Twins persisted, are you receiving this?'

Silence.

'We would like to thank you for saving the life of Davideous. Why ... why did you do it?'

'I ... I could not let him die,' a faint telepathic signal,

hesitant and frail, was borne on the ether across to the Twins.

'Why … why not?' the Twins were exited; they had made a contact, nay forced a contact from this reluctant Black Angel.

'I cannot tell you this …' the voice was getting fainter.

'Well, can you tell us who wishes to harm him?'

'It is my sisterhood, the ones who are still loyal to Hilderdrake.'

'You mean you are **not**?' the twins sent.

'Not any more. I am tired of my banishment from the realm of good. I am not the stuff of darkness…'

'That you saved Davideous is proof enough of that.' The Twins replied.

'I hope so.' The Black Angel sent. 'But there is urgent news that you should know. Whilst you were travelling to see the Oracle, Hilderdrake force-marched his troops through the dimension portal in the Caves of Thorg and has captured Maeneid. He threw a love-spell around her and holds her at his new headquarters in Merrivale, the old Temple of Jahavia,'

'**Maeneid**!' The Twins cried. 'A love-spell… what on earth is that!' The Twin's knowledge of the goings on of adults was strictly limited.'

'Not on earth.' The Black Angel countered. 'But of the underworld. For the Arch Sorcerer Hilderdrake, has bound the water maiden's heart in a web of deceit. She is held hostage to a threat…'

'What threat?' The Twins asked breathlessly.

'The threat of her beloved sunken Kingdom. Hilderdrake vows to exchange its escape from his destruction and with it the Atlanteans for the promise of her troth; her love-bond. Yet I suspect his real interest lies, not in the bonds of love, but in the Atlantean treasure.'

'How could this all happen so soon... we were only gone a few days...'

'Time is of no consequence in this world.' The Black Angel stated. 'But there is hope. The ancient Queen of the Lamaphroighs has returned.'

'You mean Mrs. Mandrake, the Gypsy Queen who...'

'That is the one. But she is not as you saw her. Beset by rage at Hilderdrake's rejection of her, thinking his recent capture of Maeneid was a genuine affair of the heart... and also suffering inconsolable sorrow at the loss of her favourite child, Rockpile... she has mutated into her ancient incarnation of Dragondrake. She has resurrected her ancient anima of the Cockatrice and vows revenge on Hilderdrake...'

'**What in Heaven's name is a Cockatrice**?' The Twins asked.

'It is a basilisk.' The dark spirit replied. 'It is a salamander or giant crested lizard that deals death through its eyes and ejects a virulent poison from its tail. It is a creature of great horror and hidden powers.'

'So ... so how can we help Maeneid?' the Twins were getting tired, their thought signals sounding desperate.

'It is too late,' the Black Angel sent. 'Even now Maeneid is held against her will at Hilderdrake's stronghold, the Old Temple of Jahavia, and the creature Dragondrake and her army of Lamaphroighs loyal to her gather on Scollock Edge to lay siege against her former Lord and lover.'

'How do you know all of this?'

'I can see it,' the Black Angel returned. 'Through our network of spies, which are everywhere, we build up composite pictures of life … and death. Yet I am weary. I tire of this darkness, this subterfuge, flitting around in the shadows … I long for the light.'

'Then leave!' the Twins exclaimed. 'Give up this nether world.'

'I cannot … I am locked in here … doomed to remain for eternity … I must stop now and rest. I am drained. Goodbye.'

'Wait, wait,' the Twins sent. 'What is your name?'

'I am called Minwa,' the voice faded.

The connection went dead and the Twins suddenly became aware of three faces staring intently at them.

'What was all that about?' Socrates said. 'You looked too busy to be just communicating with yourselves.'

'We have been communicating with the Black Angel,' the Twins replied.

'What … are you mad?' Socrates looked demented. 'Do you know how treacherous those lost souls are?'

'But this one is different. She has had enough of wandering and doing evil deeds ... we sense it. She is not lying. But she has imparted to us much of what you feared for the future. Though you cannot foretell the future anymore, you had prescient thoughts that boded ill.'

'That is so,' Socrates looked reflective, cupping his face in one strong hand as he regarded the Twins. 'So are you going to tell us what the Black Angel said, or do we play guessing games?'

The Twins told Socrates everything Minwa had related to them and when they had finished there was a long silence.

'So,' Socrates said at last, 'it seems that this little Kingdom of Merrivale is visited once more by the plague of war and by the same despot...Hilderdrake. But that Maeneid has been deceived by him in matters of the heart is difficult to believe for surely she had knowledge of his false character. And yet, and yet these things happen, and the heart is not always the brother of reason in matters of love. But that the witch called Mandrake, who has been living incognito in this Kingdom for countless years as the Gipsy Queen Sivelus Mandrake, has now reverted to her ancient and hideous incarnation of Dragondrake ... that is beyond belief, for it will cause untold suffering in this simple land.

'And to think that all this should happen immediately after you persuaded me to forsake my profession ... Why I would be in high demand now. Think of all the soldiers who would wish to consult me as an Oracle!'

'Don't be an oaf!' Gerard interrupted. 'You would be in the front line of battle. Why, the Forum of the Oracle is no doubt flattened already, or turned into a fort.'

'Oh,' Socrates looked surprised. 'No sympathy then ... And where did you derive your knowledge of warfare from... stealing fighting men's purses?'

'**Enough!**' shouted Davideous, his voice shaking with anger. 'Did you effect your own release from an eternity of worthless rhetoric and bring mine about as an act of charity, to so become embroiled in useless argument. You are like two old crones arguing about who shall jump in the grave first!'

'You are right,' Socrates said after a while, offering his hand to Gerard. 'It's just that this new world is confusing. There are so many choices ... and to be alive is far more complex than being a statue.'

'That is true,' Davideous agreed. And that is why we should make the most of it ... and decide where our allegiance lies.'

'Surely it lies with Maeneid,' the Twins retorted promptly. 'She is the innocent party ... deceived by a four thousand year old seducer ... I wonder what he looks like, never mind the lizard lady.'

'Oh, he is handsome enough,' Socrates scratched his chin under his beard. 'On the outside that is. He came to me many times during his last occupation of this Kingdom of Merrivale. But to ask an Oracle to advise you how to win in battle is a bit like asking a blind man to lead the way ... I only predict outcomes, not how tos.'

'Used tos,' Gerard smirked.

'So do we help Maeneid?' the Twins asked. 'She helped defeat Rockpile and rescue the Rhymthus, and she showed us her own realm and the Lost Kingdom of Atlantis ...'

'And the Atlantean treasure,' Gerard added. 'Though unfortunately no one thought to ask if they had heard any news of mine.'

'That could be why Hilderdrake holds Maeneid,' Socrates said, pursing his lips. 'He could be here for no other reason than the glint of gold. Why, it happens all the time.'

'That is what the Black Angel, Minwa said.' The Twins enjoined. 'That his real interest is not in her, but the treasure of the Atlanteans.'

'There is only one way to find out,' Davideous said. 'And that is by going there.'

'Very well, lad,' Socrates rose and laid his hands on the boy's shoulder. 'I see that youth carries the day.'

'But are we prepared?' Gerard asked.

Socrates looked the Highwayman up and down and spoke: 'You, sir, are … the rest of us are not. I will make one little addition to your arsenal, a brace of pistols that work, a bag of powder and a bag of shot. Now for the rest of us … I will effect a quick change for us, more fitting for the battlefield.'

The Twins watched electrified as in the twinkling of an eye they saw Davideous re-robed in a leather jerkin with light electrum shoulder armour, a helmet of similar material, whilst a sword hung from his broad, studded-leather belt.

'Draw the sword, Davideous!' Socrates ordered.

'But he can't see,' the Twins argued.

'I can feel it,' Davideous said.

'No, I mean, can't see his enemy.'

'Draw!' Socrates commanded.

Davideous slowly drew the sword and the Twins marvelled at it. For at its tip, before the point, was a bright, shining stone, like a diamond. And now a similar one could be seen in the front of the boy's helmet.

'Strike me!' Socrates ordered and, as the others watched in total amazement, the youth took aim and would have swiped the head off the philosopher had he not jumped adroitly out of range.

'I can see … I can see!' Davideous cried, swinging his sword with the seeing- eye and swiping great chunks off the temple statuary and wooden pews of the nave.

'Steady!' Socrates cautioned. 'Or you will kill us all … you need a lesson or two!' Socrates turned his attention to the Twins. 'And now for you two. I do not know where your pauper apparel comes from, but it is defective for the battlefield. What you need is *circa, circa* …'

'Joan of Arc,' Gerard helped out.

'That will do nicely,' Socrates nodded.

In a flash the Twins were decked out in light bodices of chain mail, pleated white skirts and thigh-length boots.

'**That's not Joan of Arc**!' they yelled, looking down in disgust at a cross between a cheerleader and that sixties sci-fi icon, Barbarella.

'Sorry,' the old man looked a bit baffled. He then made

some final adjustments and the Twins nodded their satisfaction – one piece overalls of fine poplin, overlaid with electrum knee and arm pads and a silver breastplate. Helmets and boots of light gold alloy completed their fighting uniform.

'So where are our weapons?' they asked.

'Your hands and feet are your real weapons,' Socrates replied. 'And above all, your minds, for they together are totally terrifying!'

'And for yourself?' the Twins prompted.

'Ah yes, Commander of the Forces of the Altered Dimension ... something a bit impressive.' Socrates tried several permutations, finally settling for a silver breastplate with gold epaulettes, leather kilt and open-toed sandals and a helmet bearing a strange insignia.

'What is that symbol?' Gerard asked. 'It looks like a serpent eating itself.'

'Can't divulge that, dear boy,' Socrates said. 'Masonic Order, you know.'

'Masonic?' the Twins looked at each other. 'He does get his history wrong, doesn't he? Wonder how much false advice on the future he gave out as an Oracle ... probably caused a few stock market crashes.'

'What are you two twittering on about?' Socrates put on his authoritarian voice. Then turning dramatically, stamped his massive trident on the ground. 'Let us this day take an oath of allegiance to assist Maeneid, and above all, each other. Let us find courage in the belief that we are right ... to vanquish the oppressors!'

'***To vanquish the oppressors**!*' The pledge of two mortal children, one former statue, one former fortune teller and one incompetent highwayman rang around the moonlit ravine.

The Etherbeasts

'And now,' Socrates walked down the nave of Tabernac Temple and out onto the terrace. 'And now for our steeds ... the Etherbeasts!'

'The What?' The Twins asked as they looked out from the terrace.

'Conjured from the realm of Mythology, and yet with all the trappings of artistic genius, I give you our mystical mounts... the Etherbeasts!' Socrates pronounced.

'He does like to blow his own trumpet a bit.' Sophie exchanged telepathic signals to Laura.

'Tell me about it.' Laura returned 'But look!'

The Twins inhaled a deep breath of astonishment, for contrasted against the indigo backdrop of the steep ravine that lay stretched out before them, they saw five milk-white, winged horses.

Snorting, the Etherbeasts turned to fly towards them, their mystical wings dappled by an occasional shaft of yellow light as they flew through the angled moonbeams. Then they landed, whinnying and neighing, clattering their steel shod hooves upon the stone surface of the terrace.

'Wow!' the Twins exclaimed. 'These are magnificent steeds ... but aren't they too big for Davideous and us?'

'No, not too big.' Socrates proclaimed, 'Do not worry

about their size. You will not fall if you bear one thought in mind.'

'So what is that?' the Twins had been waiting for a while.

'Well ... that you will not fall,' Socrates shrugged his shoulders, taking the bridle strap of the nearest stallion and catapulting himself into the saddle.

Gerard mounted successfully and all watched Davideous as he felt for the stirrup. But before they could assist him they watched dumbfounded as the mythical animal knelt on its fore knees to assist the boy's mounting.

'They are aware,' the Twins sent to each other. 'They have the knowing.'

Their own two mounts whinnied, also kneeling and the Twins swung up into the saddle, a grand affair of gold and silver chasing over tanned leather. And as they did, the mythical horses snorted and stood upright and the Twins were raised up to look at their compatriots. In spite of themselves, a shiver of sheer delight ran down their spines; for these were horses only to dream about.

'Ready?' Socrates asked, looking behind him to see the riders astride their magical steeds. 'Then let us to the Caves of Thorg!'

With that the lead Etherbeast spread his wings and gracefully glided off from the terrace to be followed in quincunx formation by the other four.

Minwa, the Black Angel, was at the far end of the terrace, sitting cross-legged and watching the procession of beautiful horses take off into the sky. So absorbed had she been with these mythical animals that she had not heard three of her sisterhood steal quietly up behind her.

Before Minwa could turn, the Black Angels had carved off her wings with a pitch-black sword, invisible to human eyes, and pushed her over the edge of the terrace. Down she had fallen, desperately trying to flap her missing wings, but to no avail and she had landed half way down the scree slope. That some of the stones had avalanched had to some extent broken her fall but Minwa lay now at the bottom near the river, bruised, bleeding and looking up helplessly as the white stallions flew along the valley of Wendell Dale; none of the riders had seen this tragedy.

Trying to summon the strength to send a message of warning to the Twins, she lay there, clutching her hurting body and seeing her attackers following the formation of Etherbeasts as they flew along the valley.

'Did you hear something?' Sophie asked of Laura, holding onto her stallion.

'Yes,' she replied, stroking the fine silken mane of her mount. 'It was like a warning, or a cry for help … but very faint.'

'Minwa, does she follow?'

'I don't see her, but that doesn't mean she isn't with us.'

'Let us hope she can keep up … these beasts of the ether are in full gallop.'

The Twins felt the rush of wind press against their faces

and stream through their tangle of blonde locks as these awesome animals accelerated. The winding river below became a blur, punctuated here and there by a curve of gold where a moonbeam struck through the indigo gloom.

The beat of the stallion's giant wings was hypnotic as they hammered on the thin air in perfect time. A trance-like state was induced in the riders who sensed that their mounts knew every bend in the valley, every spire and gully as they ascended and descended in perfect synchronisation: like horses riding on a fairground carousel.

After a while, when the initial euphoria of launching off from the terrace into blue-grey space had subsided, the five riders succumbed to the rhythmic motion and were lulled into a deep sleep, secure in the knowledge that their lives lay with a higher life form, so implicit was their trust in their mounts.

So it was that like ghosts, but pursued by invisible foes, they rounded the last bend in Wendell Dale, and would have seen before them the towering Manlieve Massif that blocks the way to the hanging valley beyond. But this visionary landscape was lost on all of them as they rode their meandering course, deep in the clutches of Morpheus

'**Wake, awake**!' an urgent signal was being transmitted to the Twin's brains. 'You must awake now!'

"Aura, 'Aura, wake up … wake up!' Sophie, struggling to free herself from the torpor of sleep that clung to her like an octopus of the mind, tried to wake her sister. 'We are being summoned …warned of danger!'

As Sophie forced herself to wake she saw before them a gigantic rock, honeycombed with caves. Half way up this megalithic mass of stone wound a path and on this precipitous track were men, armed men – Lamaphroighs!

Even as Sophie watched, she saw they had been spotted. The party of Lamaphroighs that moved slowly along the dizzying path, halted and she caught the glint of moonlight on steel - they were winding something.

'Crossbows!' Laura sent, having literally shaken herself awake. 'They are winding up their crossbows!'

'Socrates, Gerard, Davideous … Wake up!' the Twins shouted ahead, but those riders were slung across their mounts' necks, oblivious of the danger below.

'Look out!' the Twins shouted as they saw the first volley of quarrels released from the crossbow archers below, and the Etherbeasts whinnied and bucked, their fiery eyes seeing the arrows heading up towards them.

Soon they were in the thick of it. A maelstrom of barbed steel whizzed by and glanced off armour and leather alike. At the sound of this, and the erratic flight and frenzied snorting of the Etherbeasts, the others awoke; but it was too late. One arrow buried itself in Gerard's thigh, whilst another sank into Davideous' mount's flank, causing the animal to whinny in terror, its fiery eyeballs rolling back to look to its rider for help.

'**He is going down**!' the Twins shouted desperately to Socrates. 'Davideous is going down … can't you do something?'

Socrates, his voice breaking, shouted back: 'I can do nothing... I have lost my powers …it is that mass of rock up ahead, it negates all force for good and those archers know it. I had forgotten about the Manlieve that renders me weak and helpless!' Socrates shouted, his voice charged with disbelief as he looked towards the towering menace of jagged rock.

'We do not understand!' the Twins shouted as a new batch of quarrels hissed up into the air around them.

'Davideous' Etherbeast cannot fly, he is in a dive ... we must go down to the bottom of the valley, stick together!' Gerard shouted.

'Very well,' Socrates reigned in his lead horse and plunged down into the indigo ravine after Davideous, followed by the others.

They saw the wounded Etherbeast lying on a grassy spur by the winding river. Socrates landed and then the others, Gerard limping, a quarrel sticking out of his thigh.

'By all the Gods of Misfortune!' Socrates slapped his fist into his hand. 'If only I had kept awake, if only I had remembered about the Manlieve...but it has been so long since I was in the real world!'

Davideous was unhurt, if very shaken after his plunge from the skies and Socrates examined the wounded animal and then turned to look at Gerard. 'These quarrels are barbed,' he said sombrely, 'I do not know how to remove them without great loss of blood ... and yet removed they must be, or they will fester.'

'And you cannot do any of your magic to help him as you have lost your powers,' the Twins looked dolefully from the wounded highwayman up to the former Oracle.

'Yes ... look ... nothing,' Socrates raised his finger as if to project some powerful magic. 'I can feel my powers gone, sucked dry like riverbed in a desert... it is the Manlieve, the negating power of the lodestone up yonder.' Socrates looked up to the towering massif above them, the track winding across it, a ribbon, and the troops on it, dots.

'What is it ... the Manlieve?' the Twins asked.

'It is the Marker of the Mark. A force contained within that vast rock; like a magnet, it repels all power for good. Not magic already done, otherwise we and our mounts would not be here, but any benevolent force for good wielded within its field of influence.' Socrates looked dejected.

'So who created this force for evil, this Manlieve? Who is its master?' The Twins searched the old man's face, as if trying to divine a message; but all they were reading from his brainwaves was gloom.

'No one knows.' The unseeing seer replied. 'It has always been here ... it's just that everyone forgets about it, like I did.'

'Well, we definitely need some supernatural force, some magic, if we are going to help Gerard.' the Twins stated. 'I wonder if it blocks *us*?'

'*Yes!*' Socrates' eyes lit up. 'You are not of this world ... perhaps, perhaps...'

The other three watched the Twins as they closed their eyes and locked their wills together. The Etherbeasts snorted, twitching uneasily and huddling together around their wounded brother, for they sensed some new magic was abrew.

Davideous felt his sword stir and tug against his broad

leather belt, and then, in disbelief, he "saw" it slide out of its scabbard and float up in front of his face, and then return to its scabbard.

'**Yes**!' Socrates exclaimed. '**Yes, you have the power** … your power is not negated. Now I want you to bend metal, not levitate it. The Twins followed his instructions as he carefully took the steel bolt protruding from Gerard's thigh. 'Now, bend the barb backwards until it is level with the shaft. Hold on, *mon brave*, be brave now.'

Socrates held Gerard back on the long grass, feeling for the right moment, and then suddenly pulled the arrow, staunching the flow of red blood with a handful of moss that he had peeled from a nearby silver birch tree.

'And now for our brother Etherbeast.' He repeated a similar operation on the wounded stallion, relaxing somewhat to hear the sounds of the horses change from anxiety to relative calm.

'Well done,' Socrates said. 'Now do you know anything about herbs … medicinal poultices and the like?'

'Not really,' the Twins replied honestly.

'Then I shall prepare some,' Socrates got up and walked to the bank of the nearby river. Bending down he scraped some mud from its edge and kneaded it into a pancake shape, then packed it around Gerard's wound, doing the same for the Etherbeast who nuzzled his head with thanks.

'We should rest now.' The teller of fortunes, who could not read his own, said. 'That river mud works wonders, but it requires a little time.'

Before the Twins dropped into a disturbed slumber, they thought they saw three Black Angels sitting by the river, watching them.

Some while later the Twins woke suddenly; something was not right. It sounded as if it was raining: big drops but with some time apart. Then as they realised the sound was coming from the river, they thought it was fish jumping. And then they saw them. All around them the ground was littered with arrows, and they saw that they still fell, lethally yet silently, embedding themselves in the long grass; and then they realised that the sound of 'rain' they had heard was made by arrows hitting the dark waters of the nearby river.

'Wake up, wake up!' the Twins shouted. 'The archers have found our range ... we must take cover!'

'There is no cover down here,' Socrates said. 'Unless we cross the river and hide under the trees on the far side!'

'We are sitting ducks here!' Gerard said.

'I can see them,' Laura pointed upwards. 'They are on a lower path now. They have been descending towards us. They must have been guided to our position by the Black Angels... and I have had enough of being shot at!' As a bolt glanced off her breastplate she knelt in the long grass, bidding Sophie to kneel beside her. 'Now lock wills,' she muttered determinedly. 'We are going to blast them to Kingdom Come!'

The Twins felt their combined anger stir within them, aware of the awesome force that this created, bottling it up in their minds and concentrating on the massif that towered in front of them as the Etherbeasts snorted in fear at this sudden, hostile and supernatural energy that emanated from these twin mortals. 'That lower path,' Sophie projected, 'where the archers are huddled. Ready ... Now!'

Silver-blue bolts of lightening discharged from the Twin's eyes, a nimbus of ethereal light flickering around their heads. As they guided the progeny of their anger towards its target, it formed into three balls of blue fire, and when these hit the mountain path they exploded into a seething cauldron of energy.

The narrow ledge was blitzed, pulverised into incandescent rubble, and as it dropped down into the valley below it took with it most of the Lamaphroighs.

'Well,' Socrates uttered after a stunned silence. 'All I can say is that I am glad you are on our side.'

'**What kind of magic was that**?' Gerard looked unnerved; his arm around Davideous, whose silent look of abject horror spoke volumes as did the now cowered demeanour of the Etherbeasts.

'We can only do it when we are angry or upset.' The Twins replied in unison. 'We don't know where it comes from and we don't use it very often.'

'I'm glad to hear it.' Gerard replied nervously, edging away slightly from the girls.

'Well their singular powers saved your bacon, old boy.' Socrates observed with relish. 'Now how to proceed? We need to make a move before the Lamaphroighs send up reinforcements. If we can get from here and up to the Caves of Thorg without being picked off, we will be better advantaged for we are vulnerable down here. Also we will be better placed to see what is happening on the other side of the Manlieve Massif; to see what Hilderdrake and Dragondrake are really up to. So we have to remount.'

'Well, isn't that up to the Etherbeasts?' Davideous said. 'They still sound very subdued, very frightened to me … we can't ride them if they are not prepared for it.'

'I will ask them,' Laura volunteered.

'**What? You talk to animals as well**?' Socrates looked almost jealous.

'Well they **are** animals of your own making.' Laura retorted.

'That is not strictly true.' Socrates admitted. 'You see, I did a little cribbing. That is I took them from one of my favourite schoolboy fantasy books.'

'What?' Laura exclaimed, astounded. 'Don't tell me they had fantasy and school when you were a child!'

'Ah! How little you know… the naivety of youth'. Socrates sighed. 'But talk to them if you must, and I hope you get some intelligible answers. Are you going to speak to them in Latin, or in sign language?'

'No.' Laura ignored the slight. 'I am going to speak to them in **mind** language, for I believe they have the knowing.' Laura used the expression she had heard used about themselves. 'It's an alternative way to communicate. All living beings have it, it's just that most don't know how to use it … it's an undeveloped sense.'

'Very well … see if you can get through to them,' Socrates

said a little curtly. He was not used to being lectured to by a young girl.

Laura moved over to the injured Etherbeast, stroking the fine hair of its mane. It whinnied softly and nuzzled her head. She allowed herself to un-tune the normal settings of rational thought and slowly felt a pathway leading towards another mind. Not a mind that expressed itself though words, but a mind of pure thought and emotions. Without formulating any words, she asked about the health of itself and the others, and got back a mainly positive reply. Then when she broached the subject of them flying once more up to the high massif, she interpreted several differing viewpoints, as if the animals themselves were divided. Finally the answer came: they were resolved to try.

'They will fly,' Laura stated simply and the others nodded, breathing a sigh of relief.

Soon they were airborne again, soaring up from the valley floor towards the complex of caves and fissures, now thrown into contrast by the angled moonlight that raked the spectral Manlieve Massif.

A few bolts were discharged half-heartedly at them from the stragglers on the remains of the path, who were in effect, marooned, but the arrows fell short of their mark and soon they were soaring out of their range.

'This is where we need to land ... can you tell them,' Socrates pointed to a large opening a third of the way down from the mountainous peak and Laura sent the pattern.

The Etherbeasts glided onto the uneven rock floor of the cavernous entrance and their copper shod hooves clattered on it, echoing far into the cavern itself.

'Loud enough to wake the dead,' Gerard said in his usual sarcastic tone, unaware of course of the prophetic nature of his words.

'Let us dismount and lead our fine steeds,' Socrates patted his Etherbeast. 'They have done well ... can you thank them,' he gestured to Laura, who nodded.

They walked through the cavern for miles, it seemed; but though it grew darker, it was never pitch black as outcrops of glowing fluorspar cast a vapid, insubstantial light in their path.

A yellow glow ahead had them thinking that they were at the far side of the Massif and the end of this dismal cave, but they were wrong. Instead the cavern was opened upwards by a gigantic fissure in the rock that climbed into bewildering space until it was lost in a yellow haze of light. Within the fissure, suspended from somewhere high above, hung a gigantic, diamond shaped crystal that glowed with an ethereal light, the colour of which changed gradually through the spectrum.

'**Do not look**!' Socrates cautioned, 'for we are at the Manlieve, the lodestone of the Mark. Do not look at that crystal or you will be blinded, blinded and corrupted by the very evil that has seized the hearts of Hilderdrake and Mandrake, so that they regress back in time to take the form of ancient and malevolent entities who should have perished before the ark!'

The Etherbeasts, even before approaching the mesmerising, kaleidoscopic crystal, had been becoming increasingly spooked and now their fiery red eyeballs rolled back into their sockets in near panic.

'We can't lead them through!' Laura exclaimed, feeling their inner fear as if it were her own.

'We must,' Socrates urged. 'What other way is there?'

There was no reply; for whilst Socrates had been talking and unbeknown to them, certain strange round nodules in the rocky floor of the cavern had started to pulse with an amber light. No sooner had Socrates finished his question than one of these glassy protrusions fractured, splintering shards of igneous rock everywhere. Then a hand broke through. Bony fingers seized Sophie's leg and in a flash she was pulled down and through the circular aperture to disappear from view. The others scarce had time to take on board what was happening, looking in total amazement at the place where Sophie had disappeared, before they heard her scream echo up from the hole in the ground: a scream which grew rapidly fainter as if Sophie was falling, or being pulled down into the heart of the mountain, and at great speed.

As the echoes died away, a group of Lamaphroighs (those loyal to Hilderdrake) appeared on the far side of the cavern. They were dressed in leather jerkins and distinctive black and yellow striped breeches that were tucked into calf-length boots. Flat caps of similar stripy material made them look rather waspish, as did their insect-like faces. Apart from the crossbows many of them carried, their principle weapon was a short sword. They were of medium height, wiry build and moved quickly, unfettered by any apparent body armour – oh, and they had four arms each!

A few of them caught the residual echoes of Sophie's fall as it wafted up from the hole. They spoke together in an unintelligible babble that sounded more like an insect's buzzing, whilst gesticulating excitedly (doubly excitedly if you included the two extra arms).

Then one of the Lamaphroighs perched on the edge of the hole, sword locked in all four hands, and jumped. His comrade waited a few seconds, similarly poised in an almost comical stance, and then followed - and then a third.

'**Watch out, Sophie**!' Laura sent a strong message to her Twin, concentrating like crazy. 'The Lamaphroighs are on your tail ...Who, what is that monster that grabbed you? ... Are you all right...are you still alive?'

Troglodytes Below

Sophie received Laura's telepathic message but she was wrestling with real fear now. She had been shocked into terror when her leg had been seized and she had been pulled down that terrifying hole. Still feeling the spooky, vice-like grip on her ankle she had been dragged down this tortuous subterranean passage at a rate of knots.

The tunnel had twisted and turned as she accelerated, unable to stop or slow herself – in pitch blackness and not knowing where it was leading, it had been a nightmare of a ride – but not so much as the nightmare that faced her now.

For when the psychotic helter-skelter ride had finally come to an end and she had picked up her bruised and bleeding body to stand hesitantly upright, the spectacle that greeted her would have seen any normal person off to the Loony Bin!

The space Sophie had fallen into was at first sight chaotic. It was a complex of natural underground grottoes, caves and fissures, and was lit by of all things, an odd assortment of old miners' lamps. They were everywhere: in little niches tucked away in fissures and giving only ambient light, or used in groups of three or four as main directional "stage lighting". For the place could only be described as a stage.

In amongst this apparent haphazard jumble of bric-a-brac was some sort of order. Illuminated by the plethora of mining lamps were arranged groups of memorabilia: artefacts: objects from the history books, and all about mining. In fact the whole surreal scene looked like a museum's mining display! Mannequins of miners, some dressed in antiquated boiler suits and holding pick axes and shovels were complemented by beasts of burden. These were presumably stuffed donkeys and pit ponies, who laboured against old sisal ropes that pulled wagons full, not of coal, but of tin and lead – and even silver and gold. Other mannequins were dressed in Roman costumes, indicating the ancient nature of the trade in this underground mining display.

The backdrop, theatrical as it was, was not threatening as such, but it was the fear of the unknown that set Sophie's hackles rising. For she had been dragged down to this subterranean liar by some evil force – she could feel the place charged with malevolence – but where was her assailant? She did not have long to wait for the answer.

'**Gotcha**!' a bony hand seized her shoulder, spinning her round and she felt her collar-bone crack with the force of the icy grasp.

A silent scream issued from Sophie's dry lips as she looked at her attacker who stood close in front of her. He was a mining man; his pinched leathern face was cruel beyond belief. His dark eyes bored into her brain and his miner's helmet-light shone into her eyes so that she squinted in the glare. He looked like a museum exhibit, but when his ice-cold, bony fingers closed around her throat, she knew he was alive – but only just.

'Well...sharpen me pickaxe an' pickle me pitprops...what '*ave* we got 'ere! The near corpse stared at her as though he had struck the motherlode of gold. 'Never in a month of Sunday school Sundays did I ever see the likes 'o you down at bottom 'o pit, or at top, come ter that.' His voice rasped like a pit cart with the brakes on. 'You are a very pretty girl ... don't ya know? ... I can get good money for the likes of you!'

'You ... You leave me alone ... you monster!' A deep tremor of terror moved across Sophie's body, yet she was held by the throat in a grip of steel and blinded by the miner's lamp.

At that moment there came a slithering sound and a thud; then another, and a third as the Lamaphroighs who had jumped down the pit on hearing Sophie's screams, landed. They stood there, lit by the glare of the miners' lamps, looking bemused for a while and as the skeletal figure turned to them they dusted themselves down with their four hands in a sort of prissy way and then raised their swords to the miner.

'We take ... we take girl,' one of them said. He sounded like an insect speaking – that is if insects can speak.

'No, oh no my little waspish friends, I think not.' The miner retorted, towering over them, and they looked a little doubtful in their black and yellow striped pantaloons and caps.

One approached the tall angular man and thrust his short sword at the miner's gut. Quick as flash the old miner sidestepped and picking up a pickaxe from one of the nearby exhibits, pinned the unfortunate Lamaphroigh to a wooden pit prop, the curved spike of the pick cleaving straight through his chest.

Leaving the corpse still pinned to the stake, the miner advanced on the other two, who turned and ran back up the tunnel. A cacophony of sounds like bangs and crashes, punctuated by curses, grew fainter as the Lamaphroighs stumbled away from the light.

'Well now,' the miner turned to where Sophie stood

riveted to the spot. 'That's taken care of our little invaders from bug city. Now let me show you our exhibit.'

Sophie had been sending her account of these recent goings on to Laura, and receiving her encouragement. But she felt listless, tired, as if all her powers – even telepathy – were being drained. She wondered if it was the effect of the Manlieve above, or just the total horror that she felt in the presence of this wretched miner: half man, half ghost- but a killer!

'We are the Troglodytes.' The human skeleton said proudly, as if giving a guided tour of his precious museum exhibit to a group of tourists. 'In the olden days we were known affectionately as the Troggies.' Was there a hint of a smile on his leathern lips? 'In our youth we were numerous. Not all of us were professional miners, you understand. Some were sort of part timers, others were drop outs who came to escape the hustle of the cities, to contemplate solitude and mayhap find a motherlode of gold in these wonderful caves.'

'So where are the rest?' Sophie plucked up the courage to speak.

'Oh, they're here … all around us,' the Troglodyte gestured expansively at the museum exhibits caught in a moment of time.

'But … they are all …'

'Dead, I know … sad, ain'tit? But I did my best … Made 'em look as lifelike as possible … It was the Roadies, yer see …'

'The Roadies?' Sophie asked involuntarily.

'Yeah, the Biker Knights … called 'emselves the Road Hogs

… Roadies. Arch- enemies of us Troggies, they are. Always looking for a punch up … a rumble. Anyway they came down t' pit one night and slaughtered us … all me mates gone in one evening. Didn't give us a chance.'

'Then what happened?' Sophie shuddered as she listened to this gruesome account, but in spite of her disgust at this mindless violence she just had to hear the rest of the story.

'Well, I did get revenge.' The miner sounded proud. 'Tarred and feathered 'em, didn't I'

'What?'

'Tarred and feathered 'em,' the miner repeated. 'Lured 'em down 'ere on the pretext of gold, and poured a crucible of molten pitch over 'em … come on … I'll show you the exhibit.'

With that he led the way around a mass of rock and Sophie beheld a display so sickening, so perverse, that her primary instinct was to retch. Yet she could not take her eyes off it.

Macabre in the extreme, Sophie gasped out loud, not knowing whether to scream or laugh at the scene before her that played with her emotions as if they were a line of rag dolls in the wind.

For illuminated this time, not by miners' lamps but by the headlights of giant motorcycles, a motley collection of Roadies were poised: some riding their Harley Davidsons, others watching – but all of them covered in a thick layer of tar to which an appliqué of feathers had been added.

'And now for my piece de resistance,' the Troggie said,

cranking a starting handle attached to an antiquated generator. Suddenly, from the silence of this tomb, a deafening crescendo of sound reverberated round the cavern as the motorbike engines were started up.

'Can't do wheelies now, can yer?' the Troggie jeered at his trophies, almost jumping up and down in feverish glee. 'Ye can 'ear yer engines, but you can't move a muscle … can yer? … Yer grease monkeys … yer brainless speed merchants!'

As the bikes revved, the gist of an idea was coming to Sophie and she made a connection with Laura, filling her in on the story.

'I need our combined strength now,' Sophie sent, concentrating on the manic expressions of the tar and feathered Roadies, 'we are going to do a little resurrection trick!'

Though separated by a hundred feet of rock and conscious of the negative effect of the Manlieve, the Twins locked their minds together and concentrated on a fixed idea. From the corner of her eye, even as she bent her will, Sophie saw the two Lamaphroighs re-enter the cavern, malicious intent written all over their faces.

But their telekinetic force was working and Sophie watched the faces of the Roadies come to life as sentience reanimated their semi-lifeless forms. With the engines of the big motorbikes already running, it didn't take long for the renascent Roadies to take stock and pick up where they had left off: namely the pursuit of mayhem.

'**They're all coming back to life** … 'ow can this 'appen?' the Troggie shouted, not making the connection.

Twitching slightly under the ample covering of tar, and blowing aside some extraneous feathers, the big men of the road revved up their machines and the screech of tyres could be heard as they accelerated towards their former tormentor.

'Big Jake!' The Troggie shouted, putting up his hands in a pathetic attempt to stop the rearing Harley that bore down on him. 'Stop, man ... stop! We can talk this one through!'

'Too late, old timer ... you're mine an' you're mincemeat!'

The words had scarce left Big Jake's mouth than the massive machine descended upon the miner, its half a ton of gleaming chrome and paint crushing the half-ghost to a pulp. Except there was no pulp – just the cracking and pulverising of brittle bones as the long skeletal figure was repackaged into a handy format.

'I'm happy now!' Big Jake slapped hands with his Chapter. 'Thank you for our sweet moment of revenge ... ready to go back to the big sleep, fellahs?'

'Before you do,' Sophie shouted as the bandanaed, eye-patched Roadies skidded in a circle, 'could you do the same to those two over there?' She pointed to the Lamaphroighs who were watching this new and very strange action uncertainly.

'No problem, mam,' Big Jake accelerated, the thunderous pitch of the thousand cc. engine reverberating around the cavern, and rode towards the centre of the frozen Lamaphroighs who stood cemented in indecision and rooted to the spot.

Halfway towards them Big Jake reached back into his pannier bag and drew out a nasty looking spiked ball and chain. Swinging this around his head and shouting some unintelligible war whoop, he neatly effected a double strike, pulverising the heads of the Lamaphroighs, and using the dead weight of their slumped corpses to pull his bike one-handedly into a magnificent skid.

He sat astride the purring machine, blue smoke belching from its tyres, with a broad smile on his face. 'Now, comrades ... now is the time. I feel the big sleep upon me. Let's go back to oblivion in a good mood!'

With that big Jake and his Chapter rode into the Biker's Hall of Fame, as, with ball and chain in hand, they smashed the miner's exhibit into a shambles of broken figures, donkeys, ponies and mining paraphernalia.

Mission accomplished, the Roadies shut down their machines and were re-petrified where they sat, broad grins showing through the tar and feathers, the cooling engines cracking in the ominous silence and their story going on down through the ages in the annals of the History of Mayhem.

Lifting one of the few intact miners' lamps, Sophie took one last look around this cavern of trivial pursuits, muttering to herself: 'Well, that takes care of the Troggies, the Roadies and the Phroigies ... just wait till I tell Laura about this little lot!'

At that point she got a message from Laura and stopped to help her in another telepathic exchange. That done Sophie set off along a passageway that led upwards via a tight spiral of stone-carved steps, hoping she was heading in the right direction as she locked on to Laura's last signal.

Flying Lamaphroighs

Laura looked in concern at the hole into which the three Lamaphroighs had jumped, following Sophie's disappearance down it.

Shaking her mind free, she saw they were trapped. They were trapped right under the wearying power of the Manlieve crystal in the centre of the underground complex of caves. The Etherbeasts were snorting and stamping in near panic, nervously watching the weird, wasp-like Lamaphroighs approach from either side. Then she got Sophie's message from the caves below and locked her will into that of her Twin to deliver the double power needed, though Laura could only guess at Sophie's predicament.

That done, she re-focused on the problem at hand, encouraged in the knowledge that she could still wield her powers even if in the proximity of the Manlieve.

'Are we up to taking on these Lamaphroighs?' Socrates asked, feeling his own powers at their lowest ebb.

'What alternative is there?' Gerard asked gloomily.

'If only the Etherbeasts were not so spooked, we could best them.' Davideous added not too helpfully, looking at the disturbed animal's wide and fiery eyes through the magic of his seeing-eye sword.

'I wonder,' Laura murmured.

'What did you say, Socrates, when you fitted us out with

armour? We, the Twins, would *not* be armed, as our best weapons were …?'

'Your hands and feet, but above all, your minds.'

'Yes!' Laura affirmed. 'And that is how we will do it. We have done it before!'

'Sophie,' Laura lowered her head as she sent a strong signal to her Twin. 'I can't explain it all now, but I need you to return the favour. I want you to help me reason with the Etherbeasts who are frightened again. Work with me and try to get through to them. Let us pretend we are their mothers.

'We need them to be brave and to be angry … to go up against our enemies – and there will be many. If we can get them to trust us then they will be reassured like the last time.'

As the Etherbeasts quietened, listening to the soothing messages from the Twins, the effect was magical. Each of them went to their riders – with, of course, the exception of Sophie's – and knelt for them to mount. It seemed as if the fire in their eyes was more focused: not the look of fear, but more of battle.

'Come,' Davideous was the first to mount, holding his seeing-eye sword in front of him and urging his steed to bear down on the Lamaphroighs. 'Come … let us dispense some justice!'

Davideous charged down the cavern, the others following closely, the ruby-red eyes and flaring nostrils of the Etherbeasts striking terror into the Lamaphroighs, who threw down their weapons and ran.

Davideous reigned in his mythical beast at the cavern's far end and his face was triumphant. 'Routed!' he raised his sword on high. 'Fear is not the Lamaphroighs' ally!'

'Bravo!' Socrates exclaimed, joining Davideous on his mount. 'And brave of heart. Yet I fear it is the magic of the unknown that causes them to flee. They have never seen these Etherbeasts close up, nor have they been attacked by a blind boy. But I fear they will be back!'

'Then we must prepare,' Gerard said. 'Be ready for them next time they show themselves. We must press onwards and find the way out of these caves of Thorg.'

'What about Sophie?' Laura looked concerned, sitting astride her mount and holding the reigns of Sophie's Etherbeast. Had they forgotten her sister had been dragged down by some creature into some other level? Even though she had had messages from her and sent her dual will to help her, Sophie had been unable to send any details of the trouble she was in, or indeed any picture she was seeing of her place of torment; she was too busy fighting off her attackers, Laura deduced.

'Can you not locate her with your mind?' Socrates asked.

'I can send her a sort of homing beacon,' Laura replied. 'But whether physically she would be able to locate us ... it depends on where all these passages lead to ...'

'Then rather than stay here and wait for the Lamaphroighs, let us progress to the northern side of the Manlieve Massif and you send out your signal as we go, and with any luck Sophie will trace it and follow us.'

'Very well,' Laura agreed, although she felt very guilty about leaving the spot where Sophie had disappeared. She did think it unlikely though that her twin would suddenly pop up from out of that tiny hole. Leading Sophie's Etherbeast she followed the others into a long winding passage, sending her telepathic signal and from time to time receiving one back, albeit a very faint one.

The rhythmic clatter of the steel-shod hooves of the Etherbeasts was having a soporific effect on Laura as she lagged behind, sleep pressing on her heavy eyelids.

The continuous transmitting of her signal had drained her to the extent that she had fallen into a sort of coma, half awake, half asleep. Unaware of this, Socrates, Gerard and Davideous rode on blithely, not seeing the distance between them widening as Laura's mount lagged behind, hindered to some extent by trailing Sophie's Etherbeast.

Then Laura suddenly jolted into consciousness, aware instinctively of danger; but it was too late. With the lead party out of sight around a bend, Laura was yanked off her steed by a group of Lamaphroighs who had been waiting for their chance.

A leather-gloved hand was clapped over her mouth and Laura was held tightly in the grip of the other three arms as she struggled with the detestable wasp-man; seeing his insect-like face up close was a nightmare of utter revulsion and horror. The other Lamaphroighs attempted to quieten the two Etherbeasts, soothing them in an unintelligible tongue, which after a while, worked.

Before Laura could summon her powers, or recover from the traumatic shock of being held by one of these revolting mutants, a sword was placed against her neck and she and the two Etherbeasts were led off down another tunnel. By the time Socrates and the others realised Laura was not with them, and they had back-tracked, calling out her name, it was too late; the tunnel they were looking at was empty.

With the Lamaphroigh's sword at her neck, Laura had but little option but to comply with the henchmen of Hilderdrake, their striped pantaloons and caps making a distinctive pattern as they urged the Etherbeasts up an ascending winding passage and their four arms looking ridiculous as they gesticulated wildly, babbling in some alien, insect language.

As Laura's mind cleared from her earlier tiredness, she concentrated hard on sending out her telepathic signal, hearing intermittent bleeps from Sophie that seemed to grow stronger. It was evident that her own direction as she was frogmarched along endless passageways, was still moving away from the Manlieve crystal, as its debilitating effect felt less powerful. She also hoped that Sophie's and her own respective paths were convergent.

In front of them a sliver of yellow light flickered through the darkness, illuminating the abraded surface of the cavern's wall. Then turning a corner, the sudden image of a massive yellow moon, hanging hypnotically over a distant landscape startled animal, human and insect-men alike.

They entered into a vast cavern, its opened end hanging atop a sheer precipice. It was like a massive Byzantine arched doorway through which could be seen all of the Northern Territory of the Kingdom of Merrivale, dominated by the stationary full moon. As the Lamaphroighs stood staring at this majestic but surreal landscape, jabbering amongst themselves, they neglected to see a figure enter the cavern from a small cave above.

'Don't turn round,' Laura heard Sophie's message, clear as crystal now, 'don't move … stay still.'

Laura did as she was bid, still feeling the cold steel of the blade at her neck as her captor argued with his cronies in their unintelligible tongue.

Before he knew it, the Lamaphroigh felt an excruciating pain in his sword hand as the implement was seized from his grasp (but without physical intervention) and catapulted out into the abyss below. The soldier slumped down to his knees, a silent scream upon his lips for his face was locked in a rictus of paralysing pain, its origin coming from behind him. Looking down at the hand from which the sword had been wrenched by some black magic, he saw the odd angle of his wrist, the bones of which protruded from the flesh.

Freed from her captor's threat, Laura turned to see Sophie jump down from the cave exit above and run over to her. They hugged each other briefly, each recognising the jubilation in the other's eyes, and then turned their attention on the other soldiers who still gazed out onto the landscape, oblivious of the recent events behind them.

Three kicks, one from Sophie and a double from Laura, sufficed to send Hilderdrake's men plummeting over the edge of the cavern to their deaths in the abyss far below.

'Now,' said Sophie, patting her Etherbeast's muzzle and putting her arm round Laura, 'now it's our turn to enjoy the view.'

Whilst the Lamaphroigh who Sophie had disarmed so effectively with her mind, sat on the floor nursing his broken wrist, the Twins sat on the edge of the precipice, exchanging stories and Laura laughed out loud at Sophie's account of the fight between the Troggies and the Roadies and the final outcome.

'And I thought you were having a **bad** time down there,' she jested.

'So here you are.' It was Socrates, followed by Gerard and Davideous leading their Etherbeasts into the cavern. 'We back tracked and found signs of a scuffle, and followed the hoof prints which led us here.'

'Well, you're a little late,' Sophie said coolly. 'Apart from this pathetic individual, the Lamaphroighs just had to fly.'

Socrates grimaced at the mortal girl's black humour, and then turned his attention to the soldier who sat nursing his broken wrist. He sat down opposite the wounded Lamaphroigh and attempted to converse with him in his own language. After a while he got up and started to pace the cavern, muttering to himself as if trying to work something out.

'From what this fellow says, it would seem as we thought... Hilderdrake has broken his vows of love for Maeneid and has imprisoned her in the Tower of the Severed Mind in his stronghold, the Old Temple of Jahavia. There he attempts to wrest the whereabouts of the Atlantean treasure from her before he makes war on Dragondrake'

Socrates pointed into the panoramic landscape to a distant, yet distinctive, structure that looked like two overlapping triangles of some strange metal that lay at the northern end of the Plain of Rhan; forbidding and menacing, it scintillated in the constant moonlight. Beyond Hilderdrake's temple rose up Scollock Edge, a distant escarpment that lay silhouetted against the shimmering Sea of Endworld. Barely visible atop Scollock Edge, the grotesque mass of the dormant cockatrice creature, Dragondrake could be discerned, moonlight reflecting off its scales and the fires of its garrison like red dots at the base of the distant crags.

'I can just make out the Tower of the Severed Mind.' Socrates pointed at the distant temple complex and the Twins squinted, trying to locate it.

'Why will Maeneid not divulge the whereabouts of the Atlantis treasure if her own life is at stake?' the Twins asked.

'Because she knows that Hilderdrake would slaughter the Atlanteans. So much for his promises of love.' Socrates replied.

'So then we must rescue Maeneid … before she succumbs to his torture … and reveals all,' the Twins argued.

'That is a rather obvious idea … but how?' Socrates retorted acidly.

'We use the Etherbeasts. Fly directly to the Tower … over the heads of the Lamaphroighs … literally.' Laura blurted.

'But he has over a thousand men at his garrison,' Socrates argued.

'But can any of them fly?' Sophie asked.

'I don't really like it, but I can't think of a better idea.' Socrates gave in. 'Though we must watch out for their crossbows!'

'Talking of which, what do we do with lover boy here?' Sophie asked, turning to see the wounded Lamaphroigh who had stolen up behind them and was about to strike, an assortment of weapons in his remaining three good hands.

'Watch out!' Sophie yelled and side stepped one of the strikes. Laura, quick as a flash, sunk down to the ground and sideswiped the Lamaphroigh's legs from under him. Then jumping up into a crouch, she kicked the wasp-man in quick short jabs until he rolled over and over and toppled over the ledge and into the chasm below.

'Sorted.' She dusted off her hands whilst the others just stared, their faces a wonder of disbelief.

Scollock Edge.

The Tower of the Severed Mind

'This is a place of evil,' Socrates muttered, his brow furrowed as he looked at the approaching complex of the Old Temple of Jahavia from his winged Etherbeast.

Built on a craggy knoll, its metallic girders were formed in the shape of a distorted hexagram, steps leading up to its central triangular doorway. Other buildings of stone were situated around the central Temple, and to the far side was the Tower, rising menacingly from the ethereal white mists that streaked the moonlit vale.

'Steady, boy, steady,' Laura patted the forelock of her Etherbeast as she felt him quiver with fear at the force field of evil that radiated from the Temple below them. 'You are going to have to learn to be strong … to overcome your inner fears,' she sent her message of reassurance to the massive steed that shook his mane, snorting into the breeze of his own making as he took comfort from these thoughts.

'We will overfly the Tower and double back on ourselves,' Socrates shouted. 'We are high enough now to be out of range of the archers' arrows, though it is strange that we have seen no one…the place looks deserted.'

The five Etherbeasts flew over the solitary Tower and banked against the yellow moon, turning and gliding down to land on its circular roof.

'I do not like this silence...it is far too quiet.' Gerard muttered as he produced a coil of rope, which he tied to one of the Etherbeasts' saddles, tested it and stood on the edge of the tower, ready to abseil down to the window.

'I will go down and see if I can gain access to the tower. Once I am down, and through the window, follow me, we will search the various rooms for Maeneid together.' Gerard said to the Twins as he stood poised on the edge of the precipitous tower, rope in hand.

'Davideous and I will stay here,' Socrates said, steadying the Etherbeast. 'Go swiftly and carefully, I don't think Hilderdrake and his Lamaphroighs know that we are here, yet.'

They watched Gerard abseil down the rope to the narrow window below to prize the casement open and then disappear inside. The Twins followed, shinning down the rope and entering through the open window, seeing Gerard standing still with his back to them in the centre of the circular room.

'*So ... those of the single mind* ... your reputation precedes you,' a strange accented voice, smooth as silk, spoke.

The Twins froze in horror, looking from Gerard into the gloom of the circular room to see a man of medium height and age, dressed in a red velvet doublet, black and white striped breeches and riding boots. His hair and beard were as dark as his bushy eyebrows and around him stood twenty or so Lamaphroighs, their crossbows primed and aimed at the Twins.

'Thank you for being so kind as to walk into our little trap,' the man said, 'I do so hate bloodshed. I am Hilderdrake, the ancient titular master of this Kingdom of Merrivale, though I know I don't look my age.'

'Gerard...you let us walk straight into this one!' The Twins vented their confused feelings on the miserable would-be hero of the day, and then turned to face up to Hilderdrake.

'So what have you done with Maeneid?' the Twins blurted, looking in anger and confusion at the self-appointed heir to the throne in his ridiculous outfit and his unnatural-looking hair. Why had they been so stupid? Why hadn't they seen they were walking straight into a trap?

'Maeneid?' Hilderdrake measured his words. 'Well now, let me see ... the Queen of the Water Fairies gave me a very good description of where to find the lost treasure of Atlantis ... *after* I had helped her memory with a little persuasion.'

'*Torture, you mean!*' the Twins spat. How could this silky smooth voice convey so much venom in its dulcet tones?

'Come, come.' Hilderdrake frowned slightly. 'You, of all people should understand the power of the mind.'

With these ambiguous words, the Twins felt a cutting pain sear through their minds as the Ancient Warlord and Sorcerer gave them a taste of his true character and his real powers. 'But let us not get side-tracked,' Hilderdrake resumed his guise of congeniality. 'I have already dispatched a force to the Spire of Maeneid, there to enter into her sunken Kingdom and return with the lost treasure. Once I have it safe here I will release her and yourselves, and that, I hope, will be the end of the matter.

'In the meantime I have other pressing business ... like the annihilation of that creature atop Scollock Edge, the so-called Dragondrake, and her pathetic army.' Hilderdrake turned to go.

'But Maeneid?' the Twins asked again. 'Where is she?'

'Oh, she is here right enough,' Hilderdrake laughed, a high-pitched hysterical laugh that set the Twin's nerves jangling.

With that he was gone, and as his men followed they heard one door, then another and another locked and barred as the party descended the circular staircase, their jackboots echoing around the Tower.

'I'm sorry … I'm sorry I couldn't warn you,' Gerard turned to face the Twins.

'That's alright; you were not to know that you were walking into a trap.' Sophie replied.

Gerard nodded and said, 'Hilderdrake obviously knew we would come to the tower to look for Maeneid and he made it look as if the place was deserted. He thinks we will spend a lot of time looking for her here but if his has played one trick, then he will play others. My guess is that he is stalling for time, so we had best get back up to our friends and have a council.'

'But Hilderdrake said that Maeneid was still here…was he lying about that as well?' Laura asked.

Sophie thought for minute and then said: 'I don't know, but instead of searching every chamber in this high tower, appropriately called the tower of the severed mind, which would take ages and give Hilderdrake a head start, let us search for Maeneid with our minds. While we scan the tower for her brainwaves, Gerard, you go back up and tell the others what has happened, as they must be anxious.'

'Very well ... but be careful. I trust not this warlock wizard!' Gerard replied. Then he exited through the window to climb back onto the roof of the tower.

Holding hands, the Twins locked their minds together and tried to locate the entity of the Water Spirit. A furrow of consternation creased their pure white brows as they picked up on the mental torture Maeneid had recently endured at the hands of Hilderdrake in this gruesome but well named place: the Tower of the Severed Mind.

But though shuddering at the harrowing experiences that the water spirit had endured only some while before, the Twins shook off that dreadful episode and brought their minds back to the present as they scanned the airwaves for signals. Then their endeavours were rewarded and they received thought patterns carried on the ether; they were the mind prints of Maeneid, but they were distant and her signal was weakening as if she were travelling away. As the telepathic signature diminished and then faded all together, the Twins shook themselves out of their trance and looked at each other, simultaneously realizing the obvious.

'*It's a trick!*' Sophie broke their trance. 'It's another trick of Hilderdrake's. He guessed that even if we did not physically explore the tower looking for Maeneid, that we would search for her with our minds. For some reason he wants to keep us here together trapped in this room or on top of this tower. Gerard was right!'

'This tower is the nearest part of the Temple to Scollock Edge,' Laura observed. 'Do you think his strategy may have something to do with that monster on top of the crag?'

'*Of course*!' Sophie exclaimed, getting Laura's idea. 'He

means to use us as bait! Whilst we try to work out where Maeneid is, Hilderdrake provokes Dragondrake to attack his temple ... and we, being presumably the only ones left here, will be the first in line to feel the wrath of the Cockatrice! We have to warn the others ... we have to get airborne again!'

The Twins shouted up to Gerard, atop the tower, all caution gone now. 'She is not here! ... Maeneid is not here! ... It is another trick of Hilderdrake's to delay us! ...Let us be gone from this place!' They scrambled out of the window and climbed up the rope. Even as they gained the top of the tower they sensed they were too late with their warning.

Socrates, Gerard and Davideous were looking up at Scollock Edge in apprehension whilst the Etherbeasts shied and whinnied, their hooves pounding the stonework and their eyes wild in ruby-red terror.

'**The cockatrice has awakened**!' Socrates pronounced. 'Hilderdrake's army moves towards Scollock Edge but the Dragondrake sees only this temple ... and us!'

The Twins followed Socrates' gaze as he stared up towards the crags of Scollock Edge that towered menacingly, a dark silhouette against the hypnotic glow of the giant yellow moon. On top of the jagged outcrop of rock could be seen the grotesque shape of the mythical crested lizard that writhed in sickening coils of scaly armour, its serrated fin flaring. A convulsion of utter dread invaded the Twins senses as they gazed up in petrified terror at the awaking incarnation of an ancient and evil entity, older than time itself.

'C'mon!' Sophie pinched herself into action, suppressing a deep shudder and shouted to the others. 'Let's get off this tower before it's too late!'

'We can't!' Laura shouted back. 'The Etherbeasts are too spooked … they are too terrified to fly!'

'Can't you calm them?' Socrates asked. 'You are a good horse whisperer…like you did before'

'No, I can't,' Laura replied tersely. 'They are beyond consoling … you were the one who brought them into being … can you not reassure them?'

'No. The after effect of the Manlieve still blocks my powers … I am as weak as a kitten.'

'Look out!' Davideous was holding up his seeing-eye sword, intent on observing the Dragondrake. They all looked to see the monster's head lift up and look down at them, feeling a searing pain in their minds as the mythical creature unleashed its bolts of psychic pain. At the same time two vectors of venomous green liquid spurted from the spectre's tail, arching high up over its own army to land at the base of the tower.

A green and sulphurous vapour rose up all around them, causing the humans to vomit and the Etherbeasts to rear up in chaotic panic and jostle each other with wing and hoof.

'We cannot stay here!' Socrates shouted. 'We will be suffocated, poisoned!'

'Down … get down!' Davideous urged as his seeing-eye sword told him of things to come. 'And get these beasts to lie down!'

Before they could do this they saw the Dragondrake turn its scaly head, and with eyes that seemed to glow with dark sullen fire, discharge an inferno of belching orange flames from its nostrils.

The incendiary plume was projected towards them and they were momentarily engulfed in flame, which singed the Etherbeasts' manes and tails. The horses panicked and the tower was inundated with a deafening cacophony of whinnying and neighing and clattering of hooves.

But this last terror had steeled the Etherbeasts; for shocked into the courage of self-preservation, they pranced around the small tower, their manes still smoking, snorting now not in fear, but in seething anger - and preparing to fly.

'**Mount! Mount now**!' Socrates yelled, lifting up Davideous with one arm. 'And hold on ... these animals have turned their terror into rage ...this is not part of their remit and I did not make them to be so vengeful... I cannot predict what will happen next!'

The Twins mounted with alacrity and looked at each other with concern as each of them could 'read' the signals of hatred that pulsed from the beating breasts of the Etherbeasts.

The leader of the pack of five, who bore Davideous, was soaring high up into the velvet sky and heading straight for the Cockatrice that writhed atop Scollock Edge.

'They can't be! They surely can't be heading for the Dragondrake ... that would be pure suicide!' Sophie sent to Laura.

'Well, they *are* mad ... angry, that is,' Laura returned. 'And we all know what effects anger can have... perhaps they have other hidden powers!'

But the creature atop the crag had spotted them, and

twisting its head around with a scaly juddering of its long neck, it released a bolt of fire from its nostril. The lead Etherbeast saw this and swerved violently to the right and the others followed, the red-hot bolt of gas and flames searing their skin as it passed close.

Immediately after, Davideous' mount veered violently to the left, avoiding the spurt of green venom that squirted from the tail of the cockatrice to drop down onto the basilisk's own troops, their cries of outrage wafting up to the flying formation.

'We've got the beast a little confused,' Laura sent, a note of optimism in her voice, though Sophie was not so sure as she hung on to the neck of her mount for dear life.

'Have you any idea of their intentions, these fine creations of yours?' Sophie shouted to Socrates.

'Don't hold me totally responsible for the making of these fabulous creatures my dear. As I told you before, I borrowed a bit from history, some magical beast I saw in an old parchment scroll that I had brought into school without permission...though as I recall, they *are* endowed with a formidable secret weapon.' Socrates shouted back, his eyes wild.

'What weapon?' Sophie asked, hanging onto the neck of her mount for dear life.

'I can't remember.' Socrates cried. 'My teacher confiscated my fantasy book before I could finish reading it. She didn't think it was appropriate for my studies as we were in a practical philosophy lesson at the time.'

His words were swept away in the turbulence of the slipstream made by the very animals Socrates had brought back to life, even though his memory of their powers was somewhat diminished. Then suddenly, as if to herald the awakening of these hidden forces, the Etherbeasts' wings stopped beating and they formed into a delta shape formation behind their leader and started to dive.

'Hang on!' Sophie sent to Laura. 'We are going down ... or we are going in ...one way or another, this is going to be a rough ride!'

The Cockatrice saw its attackers zoom down from the dark skies above and raised its scaly head, its finned crest flexing and its black eyes shooting bolts of pain at the intruders into its domain. At the same time erratic spurts of the nauseous poison were released from its double-forked tails, but this did not deter the Etherbeasts.

Their speed of descent and trajectory was such that they dive-bombed through these sporadic, hostile bursts and swooping down onto the unprotected body of the massive salamander they ran along its length, their steel-shod hooves clattering on its hard scales.

It was then that the hidden powers of the mythical animals became apparent. With Socrates shouting encouragement to his wondrous, yet misunderstood creations, a subtle transformation took place. Where their copper shoes had been, bright blades of electrum grew out, the length and sharpness of them so lethal looking that the sight of them set the lizard shrieking in horrified terror as it saw the nature of its enemies' secret weapon.

A mad paroxysm of desperation gripped the lizard as it

writhed in grotesque, unworldly contortions, clawing and snapping up at its winged attackers, all the while the horrid green poisons and mind-numbing hate-thoughts cutting through the minds of the brave riders.

But to no avail; the Cockatrice's killer stare and toxic tail were no match for these new weapons as the Etherbeasts ripped through the soft underbelly of the monster. It squealed and squirmed, its tail lashing in contortions of pain and its black and formerly death-dealing eyes dulling as it beheld the beginning of its own end.

Swooping up again at a gravity defying rate of acceleration, the Etherbeasts banked and dived once more, their powerful legs clawing the air, this time their electrum knives ripping the intestines right out of the gigantic creature. The grotesque innards of the ancient mutant writhed outside its belly and then ruptured, releasing deadly green venom into its unprotected maw.

A shrill and nerve-jangling shriek reverberated around Scollock Edge as the Dragondrake convulsed in one last death throe and then lay silent on the crag. A stench, like the stench of Hell, rose on the thin air as the carcass was dissolved by its own venom, like a rat in an acid vat.

The Etherbeasts circled the carnage for a while and then landed on a craggy spire that rose from the steep ravine below, their formidable knives now sheathed, and snorting to each other in elation at their victory.

'What bravery and what a cunning strategy from my Etherbeasts.' Socrates shouted to the others as he patted the withers of his steed. 'Though I created them through the genius of my own vision and a little help from history books, their performance in battle even I could not predict.'

'Well, predict this,' Sophie said curtly, looking down at the troops at the base of the spire on which they rested.

'**Hilderdrake's men!**' Socrates exclaimed. 'The battle must be over then.'

All the time they had been 'airborne' and battling with the Cockatrice they had been aware of troops fighting below - the Lamaphroighs, loyal either to Hilderdrake or Dragondrake, who now bloodied the lower slopes of Scollock Edge. And as they looked down from their pinnacle, they could see the clutter of warfare - the bodies of the dead and soon to be dead - that littered the slopes in their thousands. Now all those loyal to the disembowelled mutation of Dragondrake had been put to the sword and Hilderdrake's army had 'won' the day.

'Thank you!' a familiar, affable sounding voice shouted up from the base of the crag. 'I knew I could rely on you to help me in my quest ...'

A stunned silence hung on the top of the pinnacle of rock as those on it pondered the implications of these sarcastic words.

'Great Gods of my Ancestors!' Socrates blasphemed, slapping his clenched fist on his thigh. 'Do not tell me...please do not tell me that we have been duped **yet again**! By slaying his adversary, Dragondrake, though our judgement was coloured by trickery, we have inadvertently helped our enemy to seize this Kingdom.' Socrates' words were laden with remorse. He had not seen through Hilderdrake's double crossing trickery. 'I cannot believe that I, Socrates, the former greatest Oracle in the land could not see beyond the confines of my own nose.'

'Kingdom?' Sophie questioned. 'You said 'Kingdom?'

'Why, certainly ... the good Kingdom of Merrivale, none other.' Socrates looked puzzled. 'What, pray tell, goes on in your little brain?'

'So if this little slice of fairyland meets phantomland *is* a Kingdom, then where is the King?'

A multitude of expressions engaged the philosopher's face, one of enlightenment finally settling to stay. 'Of course, a very pertinent question, but the King has not been seen for millennia ...'

'So where did he go ... hasn't anyone tried to find him?'

'No,' Socrates looked puzzled again. 'You see, after Hilderdrake's last conquest, some four thousand or so years ago, the Lamaphroighs withdrew and everything was just ...well, normal ... everyone just went their own way ... I suppose they just forgot.'

'They forgot about their King?' Sophie retorted.

'Not everyone did,' Laura said, a little smile on her face. 'The Rhymthus haven't forgotten ... don't you remember them telling us, Sophie? The old man who took off on your bike and flew back into our Dimension was Gorran the King of Merrivale!'

'Of course!' Sophie looked thunderstruck. 'I had totally forgotten ... Well done, Laura.'

'You say he went back into your Dimension?' Socrates'

face was a mystery of bewilderment. 'Well, he must be more of a coward than I had given him credit for.'

'Perhaps he felt undervalued,' Laura said.

'Undervalued ... undervalued? How can anyone feel undervalued if they are a King?' Socrates scratched his ragged beard.

'Yes, but King of what? His own subjects just forgot about him, you said so yourself. The man is obviously suffering from a severe insecurity syndrome.'

'What?' Socrates did not understand these modern terms.

'While you bandy ideas about a geriatric King who may or may not be suffering from a terminal persecution complex, and has definitely left the building, **and** the Dimension, Hilderdrake and his army are surrounding us!' Gerard, always on a downer, brought them the bad news as he dodged a stray bolt that ricocheted off a rocky spur. 'See, he has brought up his archers while you have been arguing over the rights and wrongs of Kingship.'

'Enough!' Socrates threw a withering look at the moaning highwayman and took the reigns of his steed. 'The Etherbeast's anger has subsided. Pity, for they would have made mincemeat out of those little wasps with their bows and arrows down below.' He looked at the Twins. 'Can you two do your little party trick ... like the last one, but wait until we're off the rock?'

'We will try.' Sophie replied. 'But if this next action does anything at all to aid Hilderdrake, then you yourself shall be next in the line of fire!'

'Ready for a build up, Laura?' Sophie sent to her Twin, and they relived all the tricks and lies that Hilderdrake had wrought upon them, feeling their anger rising once more to the surface. Then, as they flew up on their now quietened steeds, seeing the archers sighting their crossbows far below, they channelled their fury into a blitzkrieg of violent blue-silver light that hit the stone spire in the centre, shattering it into a million pieces of jagged rock that hurtled down on Hilderdrake and his troops below.

Even as this maelstrom of fragmented stone rained down on the archers, one of them released a bolt that pierced through Davideous' armour. But he said nothing, covering the shaft with his cloak and riding silently onwards.

'Back to Moonshine River via the Plain of Rhan and the Forest of Lum!' Socrates shouted. 'But we will avoid the Caves of Thorg and its Manlieve ... avoid that like the plague!'

They guided their steeds on a course that would take them over the great Plain of Rhan in the direction of the distant forest. The temple complex of Jahavia was coming up ahead, the Tower of the Severed Mind just below them. They were feeling reassured in the knowledge that Hilderdrake's battered if not beaten army was still at the base of Scollock Edge, some leagues behind them.

Suddenly a flash of inverse lightening forked up from the tower and a group of spectral demons appeared before them. Their grotesque heads and bodies flickered in the pulsing light of half-being, whilst their green scaly wings were equipped with razor-sharp talons at the joints that would have made a pterodactyl commit kamikaze through jealousy.

Then before even the Etherbeasts could protest or take

evasive action, a net appeared in front of them, held and thrown by the flickering illusory demons.

The Twins looked through the streaming manes of their steeds and saw Socrates and Gerard ride straight into the net. Too late, their Etherbeasts tried to bank, but they were caught in the supernatural filaments of the web and started to fall out of the sky.

'*Escape!*' Socrates shouted back to the Twins, his long white hair and beard tangled around his face as he wrestled with his unbalanced, toppling mount. 'You go onwards to save Maeneid … complete our mission!' With that, Socrates and Gerard were gone, tumbling down towards the tower and pursued by the green-winged spectres that taunted them as they held the net.

'C'mon! Up my fine beauty' Sophie thought sent her message to her stallion, caressing his withers and urging him back up into the sky to feel the rush of wind about her face as the powerful wings beat the air and she was borne upwards, seeing Laura and Davideous follow. They overflew the Old Temple of Jahavia, looking back a few times but unable to see the fate of Socrates and Gerard. Soon they were flying over the great Plain of Rhan, urging their mounts to be strong and pondering the fate of their comrades.

The Temple of Jahavia and Scollock Edge receded into the distance as the three Etherbeasts stuck to the ascribed course, their beating wings white against the blue-grey Forest of Lum that was coming up ahead.

Exhausted after the long ride and all that had gone on before, they guided their steeds over the familiar forest of blue spruce and came to a staggered landing on the terrace of

Tabanac Temple.

'It is good to be home,' Davideous said. 'I will prepare some food ... then we can rest and discuss tactics.'

The three sat on the terrace, eating Davideous' frugal meal and looking down into Wendell Dale and the Moonshine River, very aware that just round the curve in the valley stood the Spire of Maeneid. That Hilderdrake's men had taken Maeneid to her sunken Kingdom in order to steal the Atlantean treasure, they were fairly certain of, although they could not pick up any signal from the water spirit. Perhaps that was because she was now underground, they concluded.

'Welcome ... welcome home ... welcome,' a barrage of voices surrounded them as the barely visible Rhymthus flittered about the heads of the three.

'Thank you. But we have bad news.' The Twins gave their account of all that had transpired since they had left Tabanac Temple, finishing with the fate of Maeneid.

An awkward silence ensued from the Rhymthus who evidently found it difficult to relate to anything other than joyful news.

'And Minwa?' Davideous asked. 'Have you seen anything of the Black Angel, the one who saved my life, the one who is a good angel now?'

'That change of heart nearly cost Minwa her life.' The Rhymthus echoed, and they told them how the former Black Angel had suffered at the hands of her former colleagues, having had her wings clipped then to be pushed off the edge of the very terrace they were sitting on.

'What?' the Twins asked concernedly. 'So where is she now ... is she alright?'

'I am well now.' It was Minwa who had been there all along, only invisible. 'I was attacked by three of my sisterhood. I was upset for a while, but I am better now, my wings have regrown and I can fly again.'

'So,' Minwa reiterated their story. 'You have slain the Cockatrice, well, your winged horses have,' she nodded towards the Etherbeasts who were grazing nearby on a sack of oats Davideous had found. 'But you have lost Socrates and Gerard to Hilderdrake's demons, yet go now on your own to rescue Maeneid.' Minwa sounded anxious.

'Yes,' Davideous replied. 'Before he was toppled into the net, Socrates shouted to us to complete the mission... to free Maeneid. When we have done that we will return to help them. And then we will bring back the King!'

'The King?' Minwa asked.

'The King of Merrivale!' the Twins spoke together.

'But,' Minwa stuttered, 'but he is no longer here.'

'We know,' Sophie said. 'We saw him leave... on my bike!'

'Yes but, do you know **why** he left?' Minwa asked.

'Because no one listened to him anymore.' The Twins answered.

'That is only part of the story.' Minwa said.

'So tell us the rest.' The Twins looked curious.

'You know he had been living in Merrivale amongst his subjects, but incognito, unrecognised. He had been quite happy, as everyone remembered him in a kindly way, or had forgotten about him completely. So as no one recognized him, he could come and go as he pleased.'

'So what happened to change his mind?' the Twins asked.

'He went to see an Oracle who told him that major events were about to happen that would result in him being rediscovered and crowned King again. He was so upset by this prospect that he absconded.'

'Oracle ... absconded?' the Twins' voices were laboured with incredulity. 'Which Oracle?' they asked, though a tickling feeling in the backs of their necks indicated they had half-guessed the answer.

'The Oracle that is now Socrates.' Minwa answered evenly. 'Although he now has no memory of this augury.'

'Well, I'll be a ....' The Twins uttered words hardly appropriate for young ladies of their age as their brains chased the implications of this dilemma. 'So the upheaval prophesied by Socrates as the Oracle was ourselves arriving in this Dimension, and in order to avoid it the King used our very own mode of transport to place himself beyond anyone's control?'

'That is about right, according to my former spies,' Minwa said.

'So why did you not tell us this the last time?'

'I did not know that you would come to the assumption that a Kingdom needs a King,' Minwa said evenly.

'Is he coming back?' Davideous, who had been following this conversation, but only just, asked.

'Even I cannot know that,' Minwa replied. 'I can only see within this world. I know nothing about strange and alien dimensions that exist or supposedly exist beyond our own perfect world.'

'*Supposedly exist!*' The Twins blurted. 'What do you mean, supposedly? And so where do you think we come from, *Mars*?'

Minwa looked blank and the Twins slowly realised that she had never heard of Mars, or possibly the planets; for the constant and stationary moon that illuminated this fantasyland was to her and all the inhabitants of Merrivale, reality.

Saving Maeneid

'It is written that you will go on your own and help Maeneid,' Minwa said, looking at the Twins as they sat on the terrace of Tabanac Temple.

'Written, now is it?' The Twins didn't quite like the finality of that statement.

'Yes!' Minwa was emphatic. 'I will stay here and tend to Davideous.'

'Tend to?'

'He has been hit by an arrow. He has said nothing, but it needs to be pulled,' Minwa looked serious.

'We had no idea,' the Twins hesitated. 'Are you happy with that, Davideous?'

'If it is written, then so be it … and this so-called Black Angel is the only person, apart from the Rhymthus, that I can 'see' without the aid of the Seeing-eye Sword, as she too sends me pictures.'

'Very well then, shall we take the bike or the Etherbeasts?' There was no contest as the Twins made their farewells and mounted their winged horses, swooping down the indigo ravine to follow the meandering Moonshine River. They weren't sure how far behind the Lamaphroighs and their prisoner Maeneid they were, but they intended to close the gap.

Rounding a bend in the river they saw the spire and atop it Maeneid's tower dead ahead.

'Let us descend,' Sophie sent, scanning the place for Lamaphroighs. 'And let us be **very** careful!' They landed at the base of the pinnacle, on the small terrace by the river and led the Etherbeasts through the entrance into the vaulted passage with the winding steps. The same fresh breeze and sound of lapping water greeted them as it had the first time they trod this path.

The vast panorama of a turquoise ocean and the silhouette of the floating island flooded their memories, but of the shell that they had embarked on last time there was no sign. Instead, bobbing far out to sea and half way to the island was a boat; its sail a small triangle.

'The Lamaphroighs have a boat,' Sophie observed, shielding her eyes with her hand. 'I wouldn't have credited them with being so well prepared.'

'We can fly this,' Laura said, patting her mount on the forelock. The animal nuzzled her head and bucked slightly, causing the bit she held to jingle.

'Would we not be better to wait until they have landed, then we can surprise them?' Sophie suggested.

'Okay, then,' Laura nodded her head. 'We can wait here in this sandy little cove until they reach the island, and then ride across to the island.'

They settled the Etherbeasts down in the white sand and used them as cushions. They were quite comfortable and soon they had drifted off into a fitful slumber, helped by their fatigue and the gentle rippling of the shallow, breaking waves.

They were jolted awake by the neighing of one of the Etherbeasts, who had got to his feet and was pawing the ground and looking out to sea.

'What is it?' Sophie yawned, realising the animal was trying to tell them something. She rose and stretched, then looking out towards the island shouted to her sister: 'Laura, wake up! The boat's gone!'

The Twins craned their necks to see into the misty distance, but no trace of the boat could be seen.

'They must have landed, downed sail and hauled the boat into a cave,' Sophie concluded. 'C'mon, I feel rested. Let's make a move on these Lamaphroighs.'

They mounted their Etherbeasts after quietening them and trying to explain to them about the ocean; something, of course, they had never seen before and which caused them a little nervousness.

Once the mythical beasts got used to flying not only over water, but underground, they took to it wholeheartedly, skimming over the wavelets in a playful way that had the Twins exhilarated.

'Wonder if they would like to try surfing?' Laura sent.

'Not really the right kind of breakers, are they?' Sophie returned.

'Look! There's the boat!' Laura pointed to a rocky cove at the base of the great cavern.

They were approaching the island and could see the fluted and whorled striations of the sea-hewn buttress of rock that formed the giant doorway.

'There's something different,' Sophie sent.

'It's not floating!' Laura had it.

'Maeneid must have de-suspended it, unbeknown to the Lamaphroighs.'

'Why?'

'I don't know … but we'd best be on our guard.'

The Twins landed in the massive cavern that formed the entrance to this strange island, walking their mounts across the flat slippery rock of spongy seaweed.

At the top of the rock-cut stairs they stopped. There were Lamaphroighs on the golden bridge and a lot of activity around the pagoda.

'I can't see Maeneid,' Sophie sent and the Twins dodged behind a rock, pulling the Etherbeasts behind them and bidding them be quiet.

'Are they going down in the gondola?' Sophie asked.

Before she had time to receive an answer, she felt a sharp pain in her shoulder and looking behind her saw two Lamaphroighs armed with crossbows, the quarrels of which were aimed at the Twins' necks.

Leaving the snorting Etherbeasts and signalling for them to stay put, the Twins were escorted by the silent guards towards the golden bridge and its adjacent pagoda.

Unintelligible words were exchanged by the party of Lamaphroighs, who leered at the Twins, prodding them with their crossbows and no doubt speculating on their fate, the lecherous expressions on their waspish faces speaking volumes.

The Twins heard the sounds of gears meshing and a cable running and looked down to the central hole in the island's floor below to see the bronze gondola emerge from the sea. Expecting to see Maeneid, they waited until the contraption had docked, but when the door opened only two Lamaphroighs stepped out. They were carrying something quite heavy.

'*The treasure*!' Sophie sent, seeing a large golden casket over brimming with jewels and pearls.

'But where is Maeneid?' Laura returned, looking at the empty gondola.

The Twins did not have long to wait to find out for they were bundled into the empty gondola and escorted by the two Lamaphroighs who depressed the large lever and set the gondola in motion again. They descended in total silence, seeing the cable in front disappear through the central hole in the rock and down into the sea below. Soon they were submerging and watched the colours of the sea change from light azure to deep ultramarine as the bronze capsule bore them forever downwards.

'The Lost Kingdom, Aura … the Lost Kingdom.' Sophie in her excitement was sending their baby-talk messages and it made Laura want to laugh; until, that is, she realised their predicament.

Illuminated by diagonal bands of golden light, the temples and houses of the Lost Kingdom could be seen, fluorescent fish swimming through portals and between columns, but there was no sign of the Atlanteans.

Suddenly a face appeared at the porthole. It was a mermaid, her ghostly white face framed by snaking silver hair that floated tendril-like in the subterranean depths.

'*Maeneid*!' the Twins exclaimed in unison and the Lamaphroighs jumped at the sight of the surreal face at the porthole.

The soldiers turned valves and there was a hissing of air as the bronze diving bell was enveloped in a cloud of bubbles. Then they opened the water- tight door and Maeneid stood in the air-lock, holding a similar golden casket to that previously unloaded.

If she was surprised to see the Twins, Maeneid did a good job of hiding her feelings and she gestured to the two Lamaphroighs that this casket was the last one. They pulled the large lever and the gondola started gliding back up towards the surface.

The Twins were expecting Maeneid to change back into her human form, but she stood there dripping, her large gills and tail making her seem bizarre; half beautiful woman, half fish. The Twins, however, were receiving a message from her. Though her expression was deadpan, Maeneid was bidding them to remain silent and be prepared; but prepared for what?

The Twins became aware of a change in the light. It wasn't the gradual change from dark to light as they ascended towards the surface, but more of an abrupt change as if one of the viewing windows had been blacked out.

It was at that point that they saw it; a giant tentacle moving across one of the portholes; its huge suckers white as it gripped the side of the gondola. Even as they watched, another tentacle appeared on the far side, and then another.

The two Lamaphroighs looked from the casket of treasure they had been counting up to the skylight in the top of the gondola. Their insect-like screams of dismay were intelligible enough now as they saw the giant beaked head of the sholag glaring down at them, its hooded eyes bloodshot and hungry looking. At the same time the glass of the viewing panel cracked and a fine hiss of seawater jetted in.

The Twins' hands were seized by cold, damp fingers as Maeneid beckoned for them to climb into the airlock. They did this quickly and the door closed before the Lamaphroighs had realised they had gone. From the sanctuary of the airlock the Twins watched in morbid fascination as the crystal panels fractured and then burst inwards and the two Lamaphroighs were engulfed by seawater. As this rose quickly in the gondola, first one tentacle and then another reached in from the fractured glass to wrap themselves around the throats of Hilderdrake's men. A strangled high-pitched squeal, accompanied by a cracking of vertebrae reverberated round the bathysphere as the Lamaphroighs were crushed, masticated and then their blood sucked dry.

The Twins turned to hide their faces from the disgusting feeding frenzy of the Sholags and saw that Maeneid had transformed back into her human form. Seeing their anguish she hugged them.

'There, there,' she said. 'Human flesh to a Sholag is a great delicacy.'

'We will try and remember that,' Sophie said, trying to be brave.

'I hope you will, because when we disembark you will be in for a bit of a shock ...'

The gondola broke surface and headed slowly towards the golden pagoda. The Twins sensed immediately that something was not quite right. The slippery grey-green rock over which the golden bridge was located was running red. A host of Sholags lay flopping around aimlessly on the rock and sand, some half in the sea.

'What in Heaven's name is going on?' Sophie sounded scared. 'Where did all the Sholags come from?'

'I lowered the island,' Maeneid said. 'Before they took me down to Atlantis, I lowered the island.'

'To ... to let the Sholags in?'

'That's right ... They have done a nice job, don't you think?'

They approached the pagoda and then the gondola docked, Maeneid opened the door and, carrying the casket of treasure, stepped out and up to the bridge. The Twins joined her, looking in disgust at the loathsome Sholags lying around the flat rock, obviously overfed and well sated.

'What's that?' Sophie asked, pointing to something projecting from one of the creature's beak.

'Yuk! No!' Laura made to vomit as she recognised a human

leg. Then they saw heads, hands and other body parts lying all over the slimy rocks that the Sholags had regurgitated.

'They never learn…eyes always bigger than their stomachs,' Maeneid shook her head, then said: Come my squeamish mortals, help me with these caskets.'

Suppressing an acute desire to puke all over the mutilated corpses and body parts, the Twins did as they were bid.

Hilderdrake's Little Game

'So aren't we the brave little ones?' Maeneid said, looking at the Twins and Davideous as they sat around the terrace table of the Tabanac Temple.

They had flown back from Maeneid's Tower on their winged mounts, the Twins carrying the two golden caskets whilst Maeneid had flown on a large, but mysterious and invisible mount, the origin or nature of which she had been at pains to conceal.

She had listened to their accounts of their journey and the battle at Scollock Edge, wincing at the Twin's description of the Dragondrake's sticky end.

'So there are three things to be done,' Maeneid said, rising from her chair and pacing the terrace, the occasional scattering of moonbeams dappling her gossamer gown and long fine silver hair. 'Firstly, we must free your two colleagues …'

'Socrates and Gerard,' Davideous prompted.

'Just so,' Maeneid smiled at the blind boy. 'Secondly, we must defeat Hilderdrake, and lastly we must bring back the King.'

'How?' Davideous asked. 'He is not in this Dimension.'

'We will cross that bridge when we come to it, if you will pardon the pun, but I think this little lot will go a long way to persuading him.' Maeneid pointed with her bare foot at the two caskets sitting on the table.

'But that treasure belongs to the Atlanteans,' Sophie stated.

'It did,' Maeneid explained. 'But they asked me, that if I was to escape the Lamaphroighs, to give it to the people of Merrivale. They have no use for it in their sunken Kingdom ... why, there is nothing to spend it on. Anyway, they said it has caused them nothing but grief since they were given it by the Phoenicians some several millennia ago. And they are right, for they have been attacked twice because of it.'

'So it is a bribe to bring back the King?' Sophie persisted.

'**No**!' Maeneid's voice rose an octave. 'For once and for all ... No! Do they not teach you any manners in your questionable Dimension? This so called treasure is to give the subjects of Merrivale a fresh start. Yes, it will be the King's, but he must distribute it fairly ...'

'Or you will show him how ...' the hint of a smirk creased up Sophie's face.

'Come here, child, and I will show **you** how ... I will box your ears!'

Maeneid made a pretend chase around the terrace and the Twins squealed in delight, only semi-conscious of the mother figure they had found in this mischievous yet benevolent water spirit.

Whilst the three were playing, and unbeknown to them, a half-figure slipped through the shadows, the moonbeams shedding only nominal light on her sylph-like figure. She approached the laughing Davideous and slipped her phantom hands into his. His smile faded from his face as he held the Black Angel close to him and kissed her invisible lips.

Some considerable time later the Twins awoke to the sound of hammering. Stretching and yawning they quickly dressed and walked out onto the terrace to find the origin of the disturbance. It was Davideous, frowning in concentration, as he hammered electrum plating on an anvil.

'Armour,' the blind boy explained as he heard the Twins approach, recognizing their distinctive fragrance.

'For Maeneid?'

'No, for Minwa.'

'What, she will come with us?'

'Yes,' Davideous said, his voice guarded. 'She will come. She tended me whilst I had a fever and she healed my wound. She will ride with me on my Etherbeast.'

The Twins nodded, the foreign tones of love's ardour lost on them.

'Let us be certain of our quest,' Maeneid sat astride her invisible mount. 'We go to free Socrates and Gerard, but above all, to end Hilderdrake's reign of terror in our country. The Atlantean Treasure we have buried under the floor of this Temple. Should any of us fail to return, each one of us knows where it is and its purpose. ***But let us not fail!***'

Maeneid commanded her mysterious and invisible steed to lift off from the terrace and the Twins followed, their private thoughts full of conjecture as to what creature the secretive water spirit was riding and why should she keep its species hidden from even themselves; for they thought they had formed a bond of trust with the beautiful woman.

Davideous on his own Etherbeast brought up the rear. To the casual observer he rode alone, but the closer one looked, and detectable only in filtered bands of moonlight that struck down into the deep ravine, a ghostly figure rode behind him, hugging him tight.

They rode along the winding valley of Wendell Dale for some time and then rose over the Forest of Lum. Soon the Plain of Rhan could be seen in the distance, its slate-blue vastness appearing to stretch to infinity. A twinkling dot of gold emerged from the blue wastes – the old Temple of Jahavia – and beyond it towered the dark silhouette of Scollock Edge.

'It will be a great pleasure to revisit Lord Hilderdrake!' Maeneid shouted back to them, her voice charged with a withering sarcasm. 'I have many a fond memory of his treatment of me and I look forward to returning the favour!'

The strange structure of the Temple of Jahavia was getting closer, its uncursal hexagram thrown into a spectral icon by the contra jour lighting of the full yellow moon that hung just over Scollock Edge.

'We will start as we mean to continue.' Spoke Maeneid. 'We will enter through the front door. 'On some unheard command her invisible mount started to descend towards the abomination of architecture and the Etherbeasts followed, gliding down out of the velvet sky.

The triangular portal was unguarded and Maeneid landed silently on the purple-veined marble floor whilst the

Etherbeasts skidded to a halt, sparks flying from their copper-clad hooves. A palpable silence hung on the thin air as they looked around in wonder. For the interior of this part of the temple was impressive indeed. A massive entrance hall led from the inverted hexagram of the open door. It was an exercise in reverse geometry in that not one pillar or lintel was on square: they hung or leaned at impossible angles that magnified the feeling of mystery – a jigsaw of uncommon beauty that was charged with an eerie menace.

In a hushed silence they led their subdued beasts down the corridor until they reached a great hall that towered up into infinity so that its upper dome was wreathed in serpentine, writhing mists.

'It is too tall,' Sophie whispered, looking at the impossibility of distance and space that seemed to exist within the apparently solid walls.

'It is an illusion,' Davideous spoke, holding up his seeing-eye sword and looking around the uncanny space. 'I have seen buildings made in a *trompe l' oile* style, but never anything like this. It is all illusion.'

'How right you are!' a silky smooth voice permeated the place, seeming to originate from everywhere, yet nowhere. Yet, disconcertingly, the slimy voice was devoid of a body.

'*Hilderdrake*!' Maeneid froze in rigid horror. 'I would recognise that fake accent and hollow tongue even if it was at the end of the world. Your persona can never mask your base origins!'

'End of the world, did you say?' the disembodied voice continued. 'Oh, how appropriate ... how apposite ... the end of the world. Yes, you must have read my mind, for that is what I have prepared for you.'

'How mean you?' Maeneid could not hide the revulsion in her voice.

'Well, don't you think the end of the world is a fitting theme for you and your colleagues? Those who are about to quietly slip into oblivion? No ill-chosen cause or quest to pursue, just the silence of the tomb.

'That you have spurned my advances is of no consequence, but that you have despatched my men in such a dishonourable way and left them to rot in your little sunken Kingdom is unforgivable. My black angels tell me everything, you know. Oh and don't think your little turncoat friend is safe. Why, she will find out how far reaching is the wrath of Lord Hilderdrake!'

'You overestimate your own worth,' Maeneid had dismounted from her invisible steed and steeling herself against this also invisible trickster, walked bravely and proudly into the centre of the massive hall as the Etherbeasts pawed the slick marble floor. 'You are just another little despot with a few jaded tricks of magic up your lying sleeve!'

'Behold, your friends!' the silken-smooth voice purred, oblivious of Maeneid's remarks, and they saw their two compatriots ushered into the vast, pyramidal-shaped hall at sword point by two wasp-men.

'Socrates, Gerard!' Davideous cried, holding up his seeing-eye sword as he went to approach his friends. The Lamaphroighs, who were escorting them, froze momentarily on seeing the drawn sword, then one of them wrenched it from the blind boy's grasp grasp.

'*My eyes*!' Davideous shouted. 'Give me back my eyes!'

'You will have little need of them, I fear,' Hilderdrake said, his disembodied voice floating around the hall. 'But you may join your friends.'

The guards manhandled the blind boy to stand with Socrates and Gerard as the almost invisible Minwa, who had been observing these events, though unnoticed by the others, leapt off the back of the Etherbeast and ran unseen to the outer wall of the great hall, there to watch and wait the outcome of the fate of her newfound friends.

'How fare you Sire?' Davideous asked, feeling the broad hand of Socrates on his narrow shoulders.

'Well enough, lad, well enough,' there was an undertone of finality in Socrates' voice. 'I think our self-styled but visually shy little tyrant means to make something of a showcase out of us.'

As if on cue, the theatrical would-be stealer of hearts and treasure, but not minds, addressed his 'guests'. 'Are you familiar with the fairy game of shooting stars?' Hilderdrake asked. 'Well, I would like to introduce you to a similar event. Your friends, the men, will become shooting stars indeed. They will free fall to the marble floor, which I think you will agree, is rather solid... unless that is, you, the ladies can stop them.'

'How?' Maeneid asked. 'How do we stop them?'

'By hitting the stop wedge in these two pillars.' Hilderdrake suddenly became visible, his dark hair and beard appearing to spring out of nowhere, his bright red doublet clashing with the subdued colours of the vast triangular hall. 'Hit this wooden block and you will stop their descent ... for their feet will be tied to a rope ... but my Lamaphroighs will be here to make sure you fail ... to be sure.'

'To be sure?' Maeneid paraphrased the repulsive voice accurately.

'Lower the cage!' Hilderdrake ordered.

A wicker basket was lowered from the ceiling high above and the three captives were prodded inside at sword point, one of the guards using Davideous' own seeing-eye sword, which he had taken a fancy to.

'Raise them up!' Hilderdrake commanded, a tone of self-satisfaction in his voice that he couldn't disguise.

'And you thought up this game all on your own?' Maeneid could not disguise the contempt and loathing she felt for this man who had deceived her heart.

'Yes.' Hilderdrake stroked his beard as if he was massaging his own ego. 'Yes, I thought it up. And unfortunately for you, the odds of keeping your friends with their heads intact are very unfavourable. However, there is a way out.'

'And what would that be?' Maeneid asked.

'By surrendering to me the treasure of the Atlanteans that you have hidden in the temple in the valley.'

'How do you know this?' Maeneid was taken aback.

'I have my spies,' Hilderdrake hissed. 'My little Black Angels.'

'***No!***' Maeneid was adamant.

'Then I shall have my soldiers rip that unedifying temple to ribbons!' Hilderdrake stormed. 'If I cannot have you … I **will** have the treasure! Now go and play this little game and when you come to your senses you will realise there is only one way forward … for you to surrender the treasure of the Atlanteans and then to surrender yourself to me!

'Oh, and think not any of you to use your unorthodox but puny powers … they are voided in this temple!'

'***Play!***' Maeneid turned from the self proclaimed, puny little despot, her face grim. 'Let us play this game!' Though her mind appeared to dwell on the forthcoming 'game', the images the Twins received in a sudden flash were a frightening mixture of mayhem, death and destruction, in which Hilderdrake was the main recipient.

Socrates, Gerard and Davideous had been hoisted up in the wicker cage. They now looked down on the three young women who could save them. If they were savouring the dramatic irony of the situation, no such expression showed on their faces that were gaunt and blanched.

'Let us try out the old man first,' Hilderdrake shouted up to the three in the wicker cage. 'Let us see if millennia of reading the future augurs well for his own fate … a spectacular yet not oracular fall from grace indeed!' Hilderdrake's effeminate laughter at his own wit, the pathetic use of verbal clichés, echoed around the great hall.

'Ready the trapdoor … and release!'

Maeneid and the Twins watched in horror as the wicker gate below Socrates' feet fell open and he plunged out, the friction of the coiled rope attached to his foot turning his body so that his head now plummeted towards the marble floor.

'*Quick!*' Maeneid broke the terrible inertia and ran towards one of the jamming posts whilst indicating for the Twins to do the same to the other. The Water Spirit got there first, kicking the block with her foot and stopping the rope dead, the wooden brake blocking its progress through the tackle. The rope, however, flexed and Socrates' head came to a halt about an arms length from the floor; his face was an abomination of helpless terror, framed by his swirling white hair and beard.

'Good,' Hilderdrake said sardonically. 'Good timing. So much for our trial run … now we will try it with the guards' intervention … it will *not* be so easy!'

As they watched the trembling body of Socrates being wound up into the basket high above, Maeneid whispered 'So we have to devise a strategy …'

'Too late,' Sophie interrupted, looking upwards. 'They are releasing Davideous before Socrates is hauled up … it must be the other rope … the other brake!'

All three looked at the opening trapdoor and the body of the slim youth who fell through it, his foot attached to the rope that ran through the opposite pillar. They moved as one, scarce seeing the Lamaphroighs lurch towards them and using the momentum of their run, ducked under the clumsy attempts of the guards to intercept them. All three hit the braking block with their feet at the same time as the rope stopped dead once more, leaving ample room for the lighter body of Davideous to stretch the rope and stop some distance from the marble floor.

'Courage, my friend,' Maeneid pushed back the tangle of brown hair from the blind boy's face, 'We will get you out of this little mess.'

'Minwa,' Davideous cried out as he was hauled back up to the wicker cage, but there was no sign of the Black Angel.

'Now let us try **two** at a time,' Hilderdrake's voice floated about the hall. 'Use the second trapdoor!' The guards up in the wicker cage grunted some signal of compliance and readied their victims for release.

'Look! The Lamaphroighs have drawn their swords!' Laura said in alarm.

'We need shields,' Maeneid replied, glancing down briefly. 'But until we get some we must dodge them ... be prepared...'

Both trapdoors were simultaneously released and the hapless bodies of Socrates and Gerard fell earthwards. Maeneid hurled herself towards the braking post that held Gerard's rope and the Twins rushed towards that holding Socrates.

As Maeneid flung herself through the phalanx of Lamaphroighs, she felt a stabbing pain in her ribs and looking down saw the stain of bright red blood trickling down her shimmering robe. She staggered and fell at the foot of the jamming post, desperately attempting to reach up and stop the descending rope to which Gerard was attached, but in vain.

Even as this happened, Laura, from the corner of her eye saw this tragedy unfold as if in slow motion. Sending a desperate message of her intentions to her Twin, she leaped up, stepping quickly over the guards, and using their heads like stepping stones she jumped to where Maeneid knelt, wounded. Then she kicked the brake just in time to stop Gerard.

Looking across to her twin, she saw with relief that Sophie had managed to stop Socrates' fall in the nick of time, and she bent down to tend to Maeneid.

Then seizing a sword from a guard that she had stunned into oblivion with a groin kick, she quickly cut down Gerard, signalling for Sophie to do the same for Socrates.

Both Twins, now armed with swords, backed away from the guards, who were increasing in number, until they met in the centre of the hall, fighting back to back to thwart the advance of the wasp-like henchmen of Hilderdrake.

'And now,' Hilderdrake's mocking voice rang with a note of glee, 'I will really put the cat amongst the pigeons!'

'*Davideous!*' the Twins cried, fighting with all their might to protect the wounded Maeneid and the defenceless and confused Socrates and Gerard. 'But there is no way we can get to the jamming post ...the Lamaphroighs block us!'

The body of Davideous plummeted earthwards again, almost as if in slow motion whilst the Twins battled with their small but nimble adversaries. From the corners of their eyes they saw a shadowy dark silhouette fly on black gossamer wings to the jamming post. As the phantom sylph-like figure landed on the post, the blind boy's plunge of death was stopped. Davideous' body hung swinging in the air above them and in disbelief the Twins saw Minwa cut through the rope that held her loved one. She took his weight in her frail arms and glided down to land beside them.

The Black Angel was holding Davideous' seeing-eye sword in her hands that she must have appropriated from one of the wasp-men, and she joined the Twins in hacking the Lamaphroigh guards to pieces, who retreated in terror at this half-visible demon.

'Resorting to invisibility are we now...surely an act of desperation!' Hilderdrake's sarcasm resonated around the great hall once more. 'And I did bid you use no magic. So if your little renegade friend who has struck up a bit of a bond with the blind boy has quite finished, I will show you what real supernaturalism is!'

'Follow me,' Minwa bid the others to follow her as she sliced a path through the throng of guards. 'There is a door in the far wall ... and it is not barred!'

The Dungeons of Jahavia

They followed Minwa down a set of stone cut stairs. At the bottom they listened; there was silence. Then they heard the door through which they had entered slammed shut and barred.

'I hope we are not once more falling into one of Hilderdrake's little traps,' murmured Socrates, still in a state of shock and pulling his rough cotton singlet about him. He had been stripped of his fine armour whilst in the cage. 'But thank you my friends, for coming to our rescue ... eventually. You have the treasure?'

Maeneid, who was recovering somewhat from her wound, told them the story of the Atlantean episode and how they had hidden the treasure to await the return of the King.

'At least we are together again,' Davideous said. 'Please let me introduce someone to whom we should be very grateful, Minwa ... but don't ask for her story, it is a long one.'

'I see that she is someone very dear to you,' said Maeneid, smiling enigmatically at the dark angel, 'and that she holds your own life dearer than her own.'

'We have to proceed,' Socrates urged, apparently oblivious as to these exchanges of the heart as he looked ahead into the long and murky passage they were standing in. 'There is some light down here, but these look like old dungeons to me. I wonder what Hilderdrake had in mind about showing us some real supernatural stuff. I would much prefer a hot bath and a goblet of wine myself.'

'Sanctuary,' a voice seemed to emanate from the dark walls. 'Sanctuary ... give me food, Sire ... Give me to drink.'

'What kind of sorcery is this?' Socrates muttered. 'What voice from the past bids me to regress?'

The passageway in which they stood was lit by an occasional flambeau that gutted a smoky orange in its wall grating. Either side of this grim tunnel were inset cells of odd proportions, their narrow windows and doors fitted with iron grilles.

Socrates, his white bedraggled hair ringed by a nimbus of light from the nearer wall torch, peered into the cell, his face a mystery of recognition. 'Thalus ... Thalus, my old friend ... is that you?'

'*Oraculas*!' The feeble old man staggered into the light, his emaciated body a mass of sinew and tendons; not one ounce of flesh was upon him.

'Thalus,' Socrates voice took on a distant sound, as if he was remembering days long gone, 'what happened to you ... what happened?'

'I fought, Oraculas, I fought for the King. But we were beaten ... outnumbered and beaten by magic.'

'You mean the battle of ... the *ancient* battle of Scollock Edge?'

'That was it, my friend.'

'But,' Socrates' eyes were wide in a confusion, 'that was

thousands of years ago ... how come you live yet?'

'I imbibed.' Thalus' eyes lit up. 'I drank of the Waters of Eternal Life ...'

'Just so,' Socrates' eyes raked that of his old colleague, his comrade-at-arms.

'And you?' Thalus asked. 'How is it you still live?'

'I ... I became an Oracle,' Socrates replied.

'**Your destiny**!' Thalus' eyes burned. 'We told you at Academy that you were not clever enough to become a scholar, a philosopher... but an Oracle, a teller of the future, a sayer of untruths... yes my old friend, that was **you**!'

'Do you come with us now?' Socrates asked.

'Whither bound?'

'We know not.'

'Then I come,' Thalus said, squeezing his raggedy skin and bones of a body through the metal bars of the grille. 'I have long been able to escape, yet not sure where to escape to!'

'Do you know these caverns, friend?' Socrates queried.

'Only the way to the torture chamber... but they don't bother with that any more. Besides, all of my old torturers are dead. Living longer than your enemies *is* the sweetest revenge!'

'So you *are* a philosopher,' Socrates observed.

As they progressed down the inclined cavern, Socrates

told Thalus all that had transpired since their last meeting several millennia ago at the ancient battle of Scollock Edge, including the recent battle of the same name.

'So Hilderdrake slew Dragondrake ... but with your help,' Thalus summarised. 'And I'll wager you did not prophesy **that**!'

'Correct, my friend, yet Hilderdrake is still in command and must be scheming some foul trickery even as we speak, down here in the dungeons of Jahavia.'

'*Jahavia*!' Thalus stopped dead in his tracks. 'Why, of course. Jahavia is the one supernatural who can defeat Hilderdrake!'

'And where do we find him?' Socrates asked. 'I thought he was of legend only.'

'Of legend, yes,' Thalus replied. 'But he is one of the old Gods, perhaps the only one left from the time of Gorran, the absent King.'

'So how do we find him?'

'I will take you,' Maeneid said, her healing wound strapped and bound with sphagnum moss, the cosmic elixir.

'Oh,' Thalus said, looking at the Water Spirit. 'I think it involves that liquid stuff, doesn't it. Count me out; I haven't had a bath for three millennia.'

'That much is obvious,' Socrates said dryly. 'Do you wait for us here old friend, and we will meet up on our return.'

'If return you do.' Thalus shambled off in the direction of the cells; decent food, fairly comfy.

'***Only joking!***' Thalus had returned to join them. 'I just remembered...they don't do luxury class in those smelly old dungeons, and I could ***use*** a bath,'

Maeneid and Minwa led the way down the inclined corridor and the others followed. Ahead of them and flickering enticingly was a light: a light that kept changing colour: pinks, purples, orange and greeny- blue oscillated in a kaleidoscope of alternating hues.

They turned a corner and saw the origin of this tantalising spectacle, a visual smorgasbord of colours; it was a waterfall. From the ceiling high above and shrouded in darkness, a cascade of multi-coloured water gushed downwards to fall into a pit, the depth of which was fathomless for no sound of splashing could be heard.

'***Behold! The Waters of Oblivion!***' Socrates pronounced. 'I have read of this and thought me it existed only in legend...'tis the one and only entrance to Jahavia's Kingdom.'

They stood looking in half wonder, half bewilderment at the flashing shafts of coloured water that poured hypnotically over the calcite formations. Within the whorls and spirals it seemed as if faces could be discerned, but faces of grotesque and deformed ugliness. As they looked, held enchanted by the plummeting kaleidoscopic cascade, the faces in the rock, moved; sentient, preternatural, the grotesque gargoyles started to come alive.

Suddenly and before any of the party had time to resist, the faces lurched forward out of the waterfall and arms reached out, seizing those standing on the edge of the pit. Except for the Twins, who, reacting like quicksilver, stepped back in time to avoid seizure.

They watched helplessly as the bodies of their comrades were snatched off their feet and hurled down into the pit. There was nothing they could do; they were completely helpless, not knowing what to think.

As they watched the semi-human, semi-stone faces resume their sculptural form and settle back into the icy waters that cascaded downwards, indecision plagued the Twins.

'Do we follow ... or do we stay here?' was the tone of the message they sent each other.

But before they could formulate an answer, a decision was made for them. From out of the bowels of the pit arose a writhing serpentine form, its scales of lurid green and blue, its head a grotesque snout with eyes of obsidian and a forked tongue that spat green venom. A scream hung suspended on the dark air of the cavern, the flickering multi-coloured lights illuminating this spectral serpent as the Twins' minds shut down, total abject terror gripping their spines and riveting them to the spot.

Then they were crushed; lifted off the chasm's edge by the sickening coils of this monstrous reptile that defied all natural and unnatural laws of size or origin, to be dragged down into the pit, their abortive shrieks of horror voided by the watery cascade.

Scattered, confused messages ebbed and flowed between them; the Twin's minds only half aware. Their telepathic signals were not just of fear, but of a prevalent sensation that had replaced their first primal instinct: it was one of cold. Their sensory abilities had shut down almost to the point of non-existence but the one basic thought that registered in their brains and permeated their shared mind was one of numbness - a paralysing cold like none they had experienced before.

Individually they realised they were in water, but below the surface, and with every vestige of energy left, they signalled to each other to rise up, to swim up to the surface. And the one thought that urged them onwards was that miraculously they had been released from the serpent's crushing embrace.

With their bodies numb and wanting only to sink down into the cold watery abyss, their minds struggled with the prime imperative: fight or surrender to the watery arms of death.

'Swim, Aura,' Sophie sent to her Twin. 'Swim like you have never swum before! Up to the surface … or else we will perish down here in this aquahell of non-being … do you really want to die here, before our life has begun?'

Laura, whose inert body was drifting down deeper and deeper into the icy void that filled her brain with blackness, was shocked out of her lethargy by Sophie's telepathic thoughts, and fighting to overcome the numbing cold, she now kicked upwards through the obsidian waters.

Breaking surface, the Twins looked around them, their frozen, blue-tinged faces lit by a raking white light that in its severity threw everything into a harsh contrast of light and dark.

Though it was impossible to collect their thoughts and formulate a clear picture of where they were, the Twins gathered a confused impression. As they trod water and looked around, they saw that they were in some sort of subterranean grotto or cave system: great cathedral-like arches towered above them; a labyrinthine mass of tunnels and passages striking off at different angles between great blocks of rock that glowed with the colours of precious minerals: Blue John, fool's gold, even real gold – they could not be sure.

Something touched Laura's hair and she turned quickly around, treading water in this underground cavern of gigantic proportions. A hand reached out and touched her face and she panicked, nerves shot to pieces, and tried to swim away from it.

'Come,' a familiar voice spoke. 'It is us … it is your friends …come, take our hands.' Laura was pulled up to sit on a jagged piece of rock. Then Sophie joined her and the Twins hugged each other, their teeth chattering as they endeavoured to regain full consciousness. After a while they could hear the conversation of their friends, who were also in various states of shock and hypothermia.

'We have to move from here,' Socrates said, his voice faltering. 'We have to get off this island or else we will all freeze to death.'

The Twins looked around them and realised their plight. They were on a small fragment of rock that rose out of the stygian black waters. The labyrinth of caves and caverns with their deceptively wondrous array of architectural shapes and colourful adornments was quite some distance away. But between it and them was the black water; and then the thought of that hideous serpent came back to them.

And as if to bare witness to this nauseous memory, a grotesque snout broke the surface, its obsidian eyes glinting malevolently as it scanned its prey. It submerged into the black waters, only to reappear as a multi-forked tail rose up and slapped the water; then it dived.

'So who will go first?' Socrates asked, looking around the helpless shivering group of soon to be serpent fodder.

'I will,' Maeneid said. 'I will take care of our slippery little friend. May I have your seeing-eye sword, Davideous?'

The stranded company watched Maeneid as she changed into her mermaid form, a startled cry coming from those who had not seen this metamorphosis before. The disfiguring gills and long forked tail took on a menacing aspect in this unnatural light as Maeneid took Davideous' sword, poised on the jagged rock and ready to dive into the icy depths – then she was gone.

At first there ensued a heavy silence as all on the rock watched the slick surface of the jet-black waters for any sign. But the Water Spirit had dived deep and her seeing-eye sword, which she held before her, gave her the advantage of sight without light. Maeneid swam down to the bottom of the black chasm, her powerful tail propelling her onwards. She could see no sign of the water serpent and swam around in a wide circle. Suddenly from a dark fissure in the jagged rock a snout shot out, followed by a writhing loop of scaly coils that in a flash had wrapped themselves around her waif-like waist.

The serpent's head was in front of her as she held up the seeing-eye sword. Its black eyes seemed to bore into her brain and its snout opened in a sickening oval revealing a row of razor-sharp teeth that were poised to descend on the maiden's white neck. The open jaw was right in front of her face, its forked tongue darting in and out of the shadowy aperture as

Maeneid positioned the sword. Too late the spectral serpent saw its own demise as the sword plunged upwards, the silver blade impaling its throat. Black blood spewed out of the creature's mouth as it writhed and twisted in spiralling death throes, rolling Maeneid around and around and thrashing in desperate death throes. But the seeing-eye sword was well and truly stuck in the monster's gullet and its gyrations decreased until it started to sink down into the black depths below. Maeneid saw in the light of her inner visionary powers the putrefaction of death upon the serpent's eyes as it twitched, helpless now; all form of life, natural and supernatural, ebbing from its grotesque body.

A strange-looking sword rose up from the pitchy deep, followed by a slim white arm and slick silver hair framing a delicate face of angular beauty. A cheer came from those marooned on the rock, and then they dived once more into the black waters, to be helped to the shore by the guiding hand of the Water Spirit.

The Kingdom of Jahavia

'This must be the entrance to Jahavia's Kingdom,' Thalus said, staring up at the display of geological formations in their lurid colours. 'Though I have never been here of course, only heard of it from tales of old.'

'Very old,' Socrates observed, pulling on his long beard. 'And I think we can assume from the difficult watery passage and something less than a warm welcome we have just had that he doesn't like visitors.'

The two old men led the way up a precarious pathway in the cavern, marvelling at the giant crystalline formations that were strewn in their way. The cavern narrowed and the lights from the fluorescent spars and gemstones diminished so that they fumbled their way along in semi-darkness and total silence. Ahead of them lay a jagged blue-grey shape, framed by a large fissure of rock; daylight at last.

'Lo and behold,' Thalus pointed from the serrated portal into the brightness of the misty distance, 'the Temple of Jahavia … the real one!'

'That's right.' Socrates mused. 'For the one above, the one Hilderdrake uses as his stronghold was abandoned millennia ago.'

They were standing on the edge of a ragged crevasse in the rock face, looking down into apparently endless space, for no horizon could be seen. In the middle of this glimmering blue-grey distance a structure glinted, its golden domes, towers and minarets were lit by a rosy glow as if caught by the setting sun; but that was impossible, for they were many paces underground.

This mysterious Temple appeared to float in the middle of a vast space of blue mist that itself was unstable, shifting; like the mists rolling in over an enormous desert, yet insubstantial, slippery as quicksilver.

'How are we supposed to get to it, fly?' Gerard asked, his awkward attitude not helped by the latest watery ordeal in which he had lost his persona to abject terror; as well as his wig.

'We could use the Etherbeasts,' Socrates remarked, 'but we left them in the great hall at Hilderdrake's Temple.'

'Even if we could signal them, there is no way they could get through that abysmal siphon.' Maeneid said. 'Let us hope they are not harmed.'

'And your mount, the invisible one that you also left in Hilderdrake's temple?' Gerard asked curtly.

'Oh, I can assure you ... **he** will not be harmed!' Maeneid turned dismissively from this spoilt poser to look once more at the visionary landscape laid out below.

'There is a legend I have heard told,' Thalus spoke as if in a reverie, 'of an ancient myth of the Lords of Jahavia, the Knights of the Bright Light, who would ride across a magical bridge to their Kingdom in the skies.'

'That is a wonderful concept,' the Twins spoke as one for on the instant, their imagination was fired.

'What sort of bridge was it?' Davideous asked, his voice a mask of conjecture.

'I don't know,' Thalus replied. 'I can't remember the rest of the story.'

'**It was a crystal bridge**,' Minwa spoke, and all turned to look at the semi-visible Black Angel. 'It was a crystal bridge that was used by the Knights of the Shining Light, as they were properly called, and in times of emergency they summoned it with their combined wills.'

'And how would you know of such things?' Socrates asked.

'I am the daughter of one of those Knights.' Minwa said simply.

The others looked at her as if she had just stepped out of the pages of a fantasy novel.

'And now fallen from grace,' Gerard just **had** to add his sarcastic comment.

'I have made mistakes,' Minwa replied contritely, 'as many others have ...'

'This is no time to debate morality,' Socrates cut in, 'but I wonder if our combined wills might be enough to bring this miracle of a bridge into being one more time?'

'We can try,' Davideous said. 'Let us hold hands.'

Standing on the elevated rocky ledge overlooking the Temple of Jahavia they held hands and bowed their heads, and then locked their minds into one single thought: a bridge. The Twins felt goose bumps run up and down their spines, feeling their minds becoming charged with the power of many thoughts, all driven by one goal.

A light was flickering in the blue abyss, and opening one eye slightly, Laura peeped out naughtily to see a magnificent crystalline bridge arch up from where they stood; it looked so real, so solid, that her thought power increased one hundredfold, subconsciously urging Sophie to send her own barrage of positive vibes into the crucible of the collective subconscious; this effort did not go unnoticed.

'*It has worked*!' Socrates exclaimed jubilantly. 'Focus now on the power of our combined will and keep thinking that single thought, for it has made a miracle, a vision ... though look again, for a rider approaches!'

As they regarded the shimmering crystal bridge that hovered in front of the distant spires, turrets and domes of the distant Temple, a horseman could be seen, halfway towards them and approaching.

He stopped some distance from their anchor into reality where the visionary bridge shimmered, his silver armour a scintillating brightness, his mount a gleaming white.

'**By what order do ye call upon this bridge**?' a ringing authoritative voice boomed across to them. 'On what errand do you come and in whose name?'

'On the order of sanctuary ... to seek the protection and help of the Knights of the Shining Light ... and in the name of Minwa, daughter of Reingeld!' Minwa called back. As the transparent waif's voice floated across the blue ether towards the rider, the others looked at her in stunned silence.

'What heresy is this?'' the voice came back after a while. 'How dare you use in vain the name of my beloved **daughter**?'

'**You are Reingeld**?' Minwa stammered, a strange choking sound to her voice. '**Father**, is that you?'

As the others stood in shocked silence, Minwa set foot on the visionary bridge and walked out over the abyss and towards the ghostly rider. The deep expression of emotions held choked up for millennia could only be guessed at by the onlookers as repatriation between father and daughter was enacted in this fantasy setting and Reingeld stooped from his great charger to lift Minwa up and embrace his long lost daughter and hold onto her in an eternity of adoration.

After a while the Knight beckoned for the others to cross and they walked over the ethereal bridge, following the great stallion bearing rider and daughter. Passing under the massive gates with their crenulated turrets, they entered a Spartan hall, the great stallion's hooves ringing on the stone-flagged floor.

Dizzied and confused by these latest developments, the company now stood before the Lord Jahavia, his giant frame resting on an equally giant throne, his face lined with millennia of Kingship; even so his dark eyes were still alert and still youthful.

'So you have braved the Chasm of Kraktes, recalled from oblivion by the force of your combined willpower the Bridge of Vapours, and now stand before me to ask of what?' Jahavia spoke.

'We would ask you to help us overthrow the tyrant Lord Hilderdrake and to recall Gorran, the rightful ruler of

Merrivale, so to install him once more as King,' replied Maeneid, kneeling on the steps that led up to the regal dais holding the throne.

'Well said. And it is time someone started caring about the little Kingdom of Merrivale.' Jahavia looked hard at those who stood before him. 'The jumped up cuckold Hilderdrake is no problem, but Gorran ... does he really **want** to be King? I mean, why has he fled?'

'He has lost his belief in himself,' Maeneid stated simply.

'Lost his self esteem ... lost his ...' Jahavia choked on his own words as his narration turned to mirth. Laughter, the likes of which none of his audience had heard before, echoed round the great audience chamber, its gilded columns and high marble ceiling only aiding to intensify the sound.

'Forgive me,' the Supreme Lord of the Bright Light coughed, heaving himself off his throne and pacing, his golden robes emblazoned with regal motives catching the light as he strode. 'For a peasant, loss of self worth is but another problem to ponder upon ... but for a monarch, it is a tragedy! Now why, oh why, has Gorran lost his value of self?'

'Could it be a woman, Liege?' Reingeld bowed his head, smiting his breast with a gauntleted fist. 'Could it be in the loss of a woman?'

'Lord Reingeld,' Jahavia turned to look at his champion Knight, who held his daughter firmly clasped in his arm. 'If my memory serves me correctly it was **you** who had trouble with women, not Gorran!'

'That was a very long time ago, Sire,' Reingeld's voice had

dropped.

'And yet I see that love still binds thee,' Jahavia looked meaningfully at Minwa, still held in her father's arm.

'There is no love as selfless as love for a child,' Reingeld answered simply.

'But a child she is not,' Jahavia argued. 'And a child she has not been for some thousand years. Do you not think she seeks her own love, even though she has erred in the past? Do you not think she has paid for her mistakes and should be free?'

'I do, Liege,' a tear formed in Reingeld's eye as he looked down on Minwa, his beloved daughter, the one ideal, the one concept of pure love that had kept his spirit afloat through his many dark years.

'Then release her and let her go to the one she loves, and I will release her in turn from the magic that binds her to the dark side of the world.'

'Thy command is my bond,' Reingeld took away his arm from around his daughter and fell on one knee, bowing his head. Minwa stooped to kiss her Father's brow and then turned to stand by Davideous' side.

'Your semi-solid appearance to a blind youth matters not, and yet I shall release you from that spell. You have wandered for longer than you should ... it is time for thee.' Golden flames curled out of the palm of Jahavia's hand as he released the Dark Angel from the curse that had bound her, consuming her black wings and revealing her true self: a slim and beautiful young woman, glowing in the fire of rebirth.

'Thank you, Lord Jahavia,' Minwa bowed, her lustrous dark hair tinged with russet gold, her dark eyes like almonds under thick eyelashes, and dressed in a gown of jade and silver that sparkled in the supernatural light.

'Such beauty,' Jahavia stroked his long grey-flecked beard. 'Tis a pity he who loves thee cannot see it ...' Then, turning to Davideous he extended his arm and the boy opened his eyes in wonder, looking around the incredulous assembly, finally to gaze on his beloved.

'This must be paradise,' Davideous whispered, taking Minwa's hand. Then kneeling towards Jahavia said, 'Thank you, Lord Jahavia ... thank you for your gift of sight.'

'Come,' Jahavia walked towards two massive gates at the rear of the hall, which opened, letting out onto an ornate balcony overlooking a panoramic view. 'Come, let us stand a while and reflect on the beauty of nature that many take for granted. Then we will eat and drink and plan the fall of Hilderdrake ... he shouldn't be too difficult to push off his pedestal.'

The Twins were looking out at the magnificent landscape from the terrace of the Temple of Jahavia. 'It's like a painting,' Laura sent. 'Like one of the backgrounds in an Old Master painting.'

Sophie nodded; words or thoughts not required to express the beauty of such a place. From their high vantage point they looked down onto a visionary landscape in which rivulets meandered around grassy knolls resplendent with flowering bushes and trees. Further away the ruins of old temples and palaces could be seen, either nestling at the base of eroded limestone crags or sitting precariously atop these yellow cliffs. In the far distance and hazy with lazily curling mists, was the Sea of Endworld, its aquamarine brightness subdued by the glazing effect of the sea spume, as if a painter had dragged a rag brush over the scene.

The others were busy in discussion of how best to topple Hilderdrake and sat around the massive table on the higher level of this series of terraces. Their raised voices and occasional laughter drifted downwards towards the Twins, who had excused themselves, preferring to be quiet for a while.

'Look,' Sophie sent. 'Isn't that Reingeld?' Laura followed the direction of Sophie's stare at the lower terrace and saw a solitary figure leaning on his sword.

'He looks so sad,' Laura sent. 'Let us go and talk to him.'

The Twins walked down to the lower terrace and approached Reingeld. His face was gaunt; lines of anguish ran from his high cheekbone to be lost in his grey-flecked beard.

He turned and said slowly, his voice choking: 'I have lost the one love of my life. Through all the dark days I prayed that she was still alive and that the Gods would grant me one last chance to see her ...'

'You mean Minwa?'

'Yes, of course, who other? Her mother died many years ago. And it is true, I have been granted one chance to see her beautiful face again, returned to the realm of mortal by the benevolence of my Lord Jahavia ... and yet her heart belongs to another ... I have to let her go one last time.'

'Why do you see it as a loss?' Sophie said. 'Can you not see it as a gain ... for you have gained a *son*?'

It was if Reingeld had been struck by a thunderbolt. Slowly, as if in the recognition of some concept previously denied him, his face changed as the dawning of this new idea took root. Then there was a blossoming, a renascent awakening of new life: fresh hope within his jaded heart as he seized hold of the concept.

'**Thank you ... thank you my children** for showing me the obvious. So elemental was it that I was blind to it!' Reingeld took the Twin's hands and bowing deeply, kissed them. 'I shall be forever in your debt.'

Then he rose and sheathing his sword turned to look at the higher terrace and strode purposefully towards it.

Maeneid's Revenge

'Go now and bring down Hilderdrake,' Jahavia was at the shimmering spectral bridge, bidding the party goodbye. 'And when you have done so, please go and try to convince Gorran he is not such a bad King ... Adieu, bon chance!'

Reingeld rode out onto the bridge followed by the others, who were wondering about the siphon that lay ahead. But Jahavia in his infinite wisdom had rearranged the conceptual landscape somewhat so that the party bypassed the watery chasm and dungeons and on crossing the bridge, walked directly into the Great Hall of Hilderdrake's temple. The Etherbeasts greeted their riders and Maeneid made contact with her invisible mount, but in a manner not understood by the others.

'So!' Hilderdrake's voice reverberated once more around the Great Hall as he stood in the periphery. 'I see you have returned. Returned somewhat complimented in number and yet I wonder what reinforcements you bring to your puny arsenal of magical powers? In any case it matters not for they are voided as I tried to explain to you the last time you were here ... they have been annulled, expunged!'

'Oh, we do not need such exceptional powers to deal with the likes of you!' Reingeld retorted, a lightened timbre to his voice.

'Reingeld, is that you?' Hilderdrake looked a little more closely at the Knight of the Shining Light. 'And this must be your little daughter, restored I see to her former glory ... a fitting touch for her imminent end!'

'You are well versed to talk about endings,' Davideous said, 'for it is your time now.'

'Oh, the little blind boy,' Hilderdrake's lip curled up into a sneer. 'Found our tongue as well as our eyes now have we?' He gestured with his hands and all around the outer walls was a flickering of wasp-like movement as the Lamaphroighs who had been waiting in the shadowy extremities stepped forward into the light.

'You will need a little more help than your waspish warriors.' Maeneid spat, although the glimmer of a sardonic smile hovered about her lips.

'Nice words, brave words … but futile words.' Hilderdrake retorted as he looked at the central group. 'One hundred archers … all with their crossbows primed and aimed … I think you could safely say that you are outmanoeuvred, outflanked and outnumbered!'

'Drop to the floor,' Reingeld whispered so that only their group in the centre of the Great Hall could hear. 'As soon as you see them fire, drop down to the floor … their quarrels will travel to the opposite side and with a bit of luck they will hit each other.'

'Don't worry,' Maeneid whispered back, 'I have something better…a little surprise for them.'

'Such courage,' Hilderdrake raised his arm, looking towards his archers. 'And such stupidity to expend your last breath on ill-conceived ideas of escape, when your final words should be directed to your God … never mind, it is time for the final curtain to come down!' Hilderdrake was about to lower his arm, signalling the Lamaphroighs to release their deadly bolts but he did not quite get there.

For suddenly, and accompanied by a vigorous sucking sound, his hair was first dragged upwards to be quickly followed by his distorted, terror-stricken face and finally his body, his red tunic flapping like a flag in a whirlwind.

The bemused Lamaphroighs could only stare in disbelief as their commander was hoisted up to the cupola high above, his short legs struggling and muffled oaths of abuse filtering downwards. But as there was no apparent target to shoot at, the archers hesitated, uncertain whether to release their bolts at the unseen enemy above or the visible target below.

Their indecision was short lived, as with muffled shouts of stifled surprise, their crossbows were sucked out of their hands and a similar fate to their leader ensued as they were dragged upwards. Milling around at the top of the giant dome, the Lamaphroighs in their yellow and black striped uniforms resembled a massive wasp's nest.

The Twins, like the rest of their party, gawped in incredulity at this surreal and unexplained fate of their enemies until Sophie saw Maeneid's mouth moving from time to time, almost as if she was uttering commands – but commands to whom, or what? As she shared this information with Laura they built up a picture that might serve as a possible explanation to these bizarre goings-on.

Maeneid had ridden to Hilderdrake's Kingdom on a very strange-shaped mount that she had decided to make invisible – why? She had left it here with the Etherbeasts and was, even as they looked, talking to it, giving it instructions. It was her mount that was her ultimate weapon, invisible yet deadly –

but what was it?

They had to wait for a while for the answer to be revealed, for Socrates had an idea. 'Give these little insect people back their crossbows,' he asked of Maeneid. This done he addressed the Lamaphroighs, 'Now you have two choices. One is to die an unimaginable death at the hand of this little tin despot. The other is to unload your crossbows into Hilderdrake ... *let him feel the pain of his own metal!*'

The Lamaphroighs hesitated, looking around uncertainly and trying to gauge the level of hostility that this new fearsome and invisible threat posed. Then staring across the great dome that hung suspended under the high pyramid above, they looked at their leader, who hung like themselves in gravity defying limbo; the noise of great suction cups that pinned them to the wall affording the only clue as to the nature of their invisible enemy as they argued amongst themselves.

'*Do not dare to shoot at me*!' Hilderdrake shouted, his face a mottled purple, nearly matching the colour of his crimson doublet. 'Show us your hand, you coward!' he yelled down to the group. 'Show us what terrifying phantom we are up against!'

'Very well!' Maeneid shouted back. 'And I hope you are ready for this one!' The Water Spirit chanted a little spell and all eyes were focused on the apparition that gradually emerged, hanging from the dark cupola of the dome.

A squeal of unadulterated terror rose from the wasps' nest of Lamaphroighs suspended around the walls as they saw to what they owed their precarious fate: a gigantic squid or octopus, its beak twitching only arms-length from their own faces that pulsated and throbbed whilst eyes of malevolent obsidian stared at them in a culinary fascination, great globules of green saliva drooling from the mollusc's jaw.

But defying all the laws of nature, this creature was endowed, not with eight tentacles, but one hundred, all of which were employed gainfully in squashing the arch sorcerer and his wasp-men to the glassy surface of the dome. The giant mutant's tendrils of scaly flesh coiled themselves sickenly around its prey, its beady eyes darting from one captive to another, as if the creature was reading a menu. But the mother of all horrors came when the Lamaphroighs saw the ends of the tentacles that held them aloft, for they were horrendous in the extreme, pulsating with a life of their own, and their odour was noxious.

'It's one of the Sholags, but twice the size.' Sophie sent to Laura, having finally identified the mysterious monster. 'She must have brought it with her from Atlantis ... but how? ... I thought they could only live in water.'

'Whatever the case,' Laura observed, screwing up her face in disgust, 'it stinks to high Heaven ... and it looks mighty hungry!'

Socrates was whispering in Maeneid's ear. 'Change of plan!' Maeneid shouted up to Hilderdrake and his captive audience. 'Forget your crossbows and your target. What we will play now is what is called "eat or jump" ... or to be more precise – "jump or be eaten." Our Centerpuss is a little hungry, so we can play a similar game to the one you played on our friends down here when you had them tied to a rope. The only difference is, in your case, there will be no rope!

'So for those of you who can't figure it out, you can either jump by tapping the appropriate tentacle and take your chances on the marble floor, or you can be eaten by our well mannered, but rather hungry Sholag ... now how's that for a choice?'

'Yuck!' Laura made as if to throw up. 'I'm not too sure if I like this kind of ending.'

'**Hold your positions, men**,' Hilderdrake's voice, not quite so confident now, rang around the high cupola as he tried one last desperate attempt to rally his troops. 'There's a chest of golden ducats for the man who shoots this little ghastly-faced, foul-smelling monster in his shifty eye ... are you ready?'

Some of the Lamaphroighs suspended around the cupola raised their crossbows, their hands trembling as they looked up at the horrific mutant. As one prepared to fire, a sudden convulsing of fishy flesh erupted and to the abortive screams of the unfortunate man, his body was catapulted into the open beak of the Centerpuss by a lightening coil of a writhing tentacle.

The grotesque beak snapped shut and there ensued a stunned silence that turned into a strident tremolo of disgust as the maw of the hybrid creature opened wide in a resonant belch to reveal the half eaten corpse of the Lamaphroigh.

This last act of obscenity was too much for the remaining Lamaphroighs, who tapped the respective tentacle holding them, and oblivious to the shouts of Hilderdrake as he dangled in mid air, plummeted to a quick, if not clean death down to the marble floor below.

Hilderdrake, his fearful eyes now distended like stalks, looked up at the still masticating beast and vigorously tapped the suction cup on the tentacle holding him. The Sholag seemed to look beseechingly down at his mistress, who gave her signal to him. A leering smile of gratification spread over the Sholag's hideous, salivating beak as he lifted the plump delicacy up towards him.

'I told you he was hungry!' Maeneid shouted up to the terror-stricken Hilderdrake. 'Bon appetite!'

The Twins turned their faces away from the sickening sight as the others relaxed visibly.

'Not quite the ending I had in mind for Lord Hilderdrake,' Reingeld mused, 'but fitting enough, I suppose.' He stepped carefully around the splattered corpses of the Lamaphroighs and followed by the others, walked out of the temple, then said.

'Having completed my mission without lifting a finger, though I shall never eat seafood again, I will return now to Jahavia's Kingdom. I am certain you will persuade Gorran to return.' Then turning to Minwa he knelt on one knee. 'Goodbye, sweet daughter. Come and visit me when you are in these parts and I will hear news of you ... Look after her,' he added, turning to Davideous.

Father and Daughter embraced and the entire assembly watched Reingeld ride back into the mystical Kingdom, seeing the crystal bridge appear once again out of nowhere.

'Come,' Socrates said, 'let us go back to Merrivale. Let us go and persuade our King to do his rightful duty and return.

The Fairies' Farewell

The Twins and their comrades were gathered on the Bridge of Time. All around them were throngs of merry makers: fairies, goblins and hobgoblins, leprechauns and a diverse variety of little people.

Festivities were in full swing and an area on the topside of the honeycomb bridge had been set aside for dancing to the accompaniment of various groups of musicians who sometimes clashed in their respective renderings of fairy folk tunes. This, however, did not deter the dancers who were at it hammer and tongs and a merry old racket they made.

At one end, tables of all kinds laden with food and drink were laid out, though not quite as neatly as they had been at the start. On the other end of the bridge, the end that led to the mortal world, a red carpet had been rolled down; for the fairies were expecting a very special guest.

Several entreaties had been made to the King who, gossip had it, was too frightened to venture back into the fairy Kingdom and so was hanging about twiddling his thumbs on the other side of the invisible wall. Some had even claimed to have seen his thumbs projecting through from the other side, and they had definitely been twiddling - so there was the proof.

But the entreaties made, like appeals to Gorran's honour and self respect and how his Kingdom really needed him, had fallen on deaf ears; except they knew he wasn't deaf.

A council had been quickly convened and the fairy folk had expressed numerous and diverse views about ways of enticing back their reluctant King. Some of the older people who could remember Gorran from thousands of years ago had come up with the best idea: to hold a birthday party for him. Not that they knew for certain that it **was** his birthday, or, come to think of it, how old he was, but it was the one thing that accompanied a birthday party that they thought would bring him out of his cover – *a birthday cake*!

So the cooks of the community had been put to work in the kitchens to make a cake. Not an ordinary cake mind, but a cake of regal proportions with decorations fit literally for a King. Finally the cake was finished and a massive cart drawn by two mules trundled up the nearside of the bridge.

'Gangway, gangway!' the muleteer shouted, urging his animals onwards with bunches of carrots dangling from a stick in front of their noses. 'Will yer cease yer senseless jigging an' let us pass!' the cart driver urged his mules into the dancing throng, nearly overturning the cake. This was gigantic, towering a good two arms length high and consisting of five tiers. But it was the decoration that made it a work of art. Fruits of all shapes and sizes hung from its smooth marzipan and icing surface whilst on the top was a marzipan figure of a king, complete with throne, crown and sceptre.

Four sturdy bakers took the wooden poles projecting from the base and carefully transferred the cake onto a strong table that groaned under the weight, and the muleteer turned his mules and cart around and drove away.

'Now, will yer be lookin' at that,' a green leprechaun said, coming up to the cake that towered over him, three times his size. His finger, which was about to scoop up a bit of the icing, was promptly slapped by a matronly woman. 'Shame on yer, Shamus,' she clicked her tongue and her husband slunk off to get another ginger beer.

'Hear ye! Hear ye!' a stentorian voice caught most people's attention and they stopped dancing, playing music and talking, and those that didn't soon regretted it.

'Yer scurvy vagabonds an' poxy knaves ... Are ye all a penny short o' the King's shillin'? ... I told 'e to put wood in 'ole!'

'But that means to shut the door,' some unfortunate wag was brave enough to point out.

'Don't tell the likes o' me 'ow ter speak slang, yer jumped up little schoolmaster. Cos I've bin public speakin' afore yer was sitting on yer tin potty. An' 'ow's that? Cos I am yer Town Crier ... soon to be Mayor, when our trusty King returns!'

The Twins had been watching the goings-on for some time, trying to keep straight faces. But the arrival of this pompous little man in his green and black tweed jacket and plus fours, his pot belly and ridiculous ginger hair combed over his shiny bald pate, was just too much. They burst out into a fit of giggling.

'And who, may I ask, sees fit ter interrupt these very important proceedin's?' the pompous little man's attention was redirected towards the Twins, causing him to elevate his line of sight.

'Oh, it's you. The double trouble that caused all of this kafuffle... if it 'adn't bin fer yer infernal machine with its round moving bits, the King would not 'ave fled the country.'

'Well, you can hardly blame him for wanting to get away from the likes of you!' Laura blurted. There was an uncertain snigger that went around the fairy folk; someone was finally standing up to this loud-mouthed bully Tom Cronit, or Cronit the Crier as he was called behind his back.

'Anyway,' Sophie added. 'When we asked, "does anyone want a ride on our bike" we were only being civil. How were we to know that a King would want to use it to escape his own subjects? And in any case, we want it back so that we also can get away from you ungrateful, stupid little people ...'

'Stupid, ungrateful ... whatderyermean?'

'Well, look at you,' Sophie retorted. 'The people you should be concerned about are here, all here,' she gestured to Socrates and the rest, who were beginning to look a little embarrassed. 'These are the people who really helped you: fought your enemies of old like Hilderdrake and Dragondrake so that you can live in peace for another four thousand years or so.

'Yet all you can think about is trying to tempt back an old crone who thinks he is a King and lure him back, not with a war chest of money that is here,' she pointed to the two chests of Atlantean treasure at Maeneid's feet, 'money I might add that could help the aged and infirm among you ... but all you offer him is a *cake!*''

'Well, 'e likes *cake!*'' Tom Cronit said bluntly.

'No I don't!' a gruff voice spoke from the end of the bridge, the Mortal end.

There was a rapt silence as all looked in the direction of the voice. A diminutive old man, as brown and wrinkled as a walnut, stepped through the dimensional divider and walked unsteadily towards them along the red carpet.

'I don't like **cake** and I don't like self-important people that **bray** ... like you, Tom Cronit.' Gorran looked from the ego-deflated, would-be mayor to the gathered assembly. 'And if you want to know the real reason I left, if any of you had bothered to ask me, it is because I had grown fed up to the back teeth of all this **squabbling**! Silly little people with silly little minds who do nothing all day but gossip and tell tales on each other!'

The fairy folk who had heard the King's speech hung their heads in shame, some of them nodding in agreement.

'I haven't lost my sense of self worth as some of you think. I left because I couldn't get through to you anymore. You had all stopped *listening*!'

There was an uneasy shuffling of feet and a fidgeting of hands as the King's subjects averted their eyes from each other.

'And what these two young ladies say is true. Our wholehearted thanks should go out to them and their noble colleagues for saving us from another millennia of occupation. And I ask you now to join me in doing just that.'

'But will you return?' one brave fellow asked. 'Will you return and be our King?'

'If,' Gorran replied, 'if you are willing to show your appreciation to these heroes and if you promise me to change, to listen, and not to gossip all the time ... then I will return. But I need your solemn oath!'

'We will,' the congregation of Fairy folk chanted, still looking at the ground. 'We will be grateful and give thanks and we will not gossip.'

'Promise?' the King asked.

'Promise,' came the reply.

'Very well then. Now let me award these stalwart gentlemen and ladies with their medals.'

'Medals, Sire? We don't have any medals,' someone muttered.

'No, but I do,' Gorran said, his brown tweed tailcoat flapping as he rummaged through the two caskets.

'Madam,' the wizened old man looked up at Maeneid. 'You first, My Lady. May I this day confer upon you the Order of Mermaid Immortal.' Then whispering to the water spirit. 'Can you quickly change this gold coin into a medallion... something fitting, like a dolphin or something?'

'Thank you, Your Excellency,' Maeneid bowed, her ash blonde hair hanging down to the ground though her sylph-like figure still towered over the King; she winked at the Twins and added: 'It is an honour, Sire.'

Applause, the likes of which had never been heard for a very long time in Merrivale went up from those on the bridge as one by one the heroes of the hour were decorated and then toasted with goblets of ginger beer held on high.

'Your crown, Sire,' a little street urchin, grubby and barefoot, pushed his way through the jostling throng of well-wishers. He was holding a purple cushion on which rested a golden crown.

'Where did you get this from?' Gorran asked.

'I … I stole it, Sire. After you left I broke into your Royal Apartments just below here,' he gestured down to the top level of the bridge.

'Well,' Gorran mused, taking the crown. 'At least you are honest … but you don't mind if I behead you later, do you?'

The boy looked uncertainly at the King, whose face broke into an infectious grin, his brown, grizzled features puckering into a multitude of lines; genuine antique lines, each of them at least four thousand years old.

'You're joking, Sire,' the urchin boy sighed with relief. 'But you 'ad me goin' good an' proper for a moment.'

Socrates' unmistakable voice rang round the bridge as he cried: '**To the King**!' and he held his goblet of ginger beer aloft.

'To the King!' the other voices repeated in unison.

'That reminds me,' Gorran said, looking at Socrates. 'I shall be needing a new Mayor and you certainly have the voice for it … what do you say?'

'It is an honour, Sire,' Socrates bowed, then sweeping back his long white hair, spoke thus: 'But I must tell you Your Majesty, that if elected, my first job as your new Mayor would be to appropriate some of this treasure.'

'Appropriate … treasure …explain yourself sir!'

'Well, Sire, I would like my first job to be the overseeing of the building of your new palace.'

'My new palace?' Gorran scratched his nutshell of a head. 'What's on earth's wrong with my old one?'

'You haven't got one, Excellency,' Socrates replied.

'Oh ... no ... You are quite right ... I haven't got one. Well, we can't have a King without a palace, now can we.'

'That is correct, Sire,' Socrates beamed, then looking around the expectant company asked: 'Does anyone here have any objection to this idea?'

No one spoke.

'Silence reigns,' Socrates observed.

'I thought I reigned,' Gorran replied.

A titter of laughter went round the bridge.

'Do we have any other business?' Gorran asked.

'My bike, Your Majesty.' Sophie spoke.

'Oh, you will find it just beyond the magic curtain, leaning against a large oak tree,' Gorran said, distracted now by thoughts of his new palace and eager to enter into conversation about it with Socrates.

'C'mon,' Sophie sent to Laura. 'Let's skedaddle whilst they're talking. It will take forever to say goodbye.'

Laura nudged her bike, which they had flown from the

Tabanac Temple through the milling throng of fairy folk and they walked quietly down the red carpet leading to the boundary of the Mortal world.

'**So!**' a deep voice spoke from behind them. 'Sneaking off without saying goodbye ... and you haven't even tried the cake!'

Socrates, Maeneid and the others walked towards them holding two plates of cake, carefully sliced into neat but rather generous portions. They needn't have worried about tedious farewells from the fairy contingent, for once the cake had been cut, the little people engaged in a feeding frenzy and were far too flushed and flustered to fuss at frivolous phantom fairy farewells.

'Will you come back and see us?' Socrates asked.

'Yes, come back, come back, return, return,' the multiple voices of the Rhymthus echoed.

'Rhymthus,' the Twins voiced their delight. 'Will you bring us in again; will you guide us to the bridge?'

'We will ... we will,' the Rhymthus replied.

'You **have** to come,' Davideous said, holding Minwa close. 'You have to come to our wedding!'

'**Your wedding**?' the Twins exclaimed.

'Yes. We will be married soon.'

'How shall we know the date?'

'Look for a sign,' Gerard said. 'I will post it up on the old oak tree.'

'So it was **you!**' the Twins gawped. 'Why did **you** lure us into this time warp?'

'Because I thought with your peculiar powers that you would be able to help me locate my stolen treasure,' the Highwayman's voice had a shrill edge of desperation to it.

'**For the love of the Great God Jahavia**!' Socrates blasphemed. 'Can somebody, **anybody**, help this man find his stolen treasure!'

'I will,' a voice shouted. 'I will ... and me ... me too!'

'There you are, my old friend,' Socrates slapped the perpetually disgruntled Highwayman on the back. 'And when one of 'em finds it don't forget to give him a fair sized tip!'

'And was it you who placed our fairy bracelets in the magpie's nest?' The Twins asked of the crestfallen Gerard.

'No...it was us.' The Rhymthus laughed. 'We borrowed them from Sammy, the street urchin who stole them from the King's chambers.'

'So they belong to the King.' The Twins fiddled with their fairy bracelets.

'Keep them.' Maeneid spoke. 'The King would want you to have them. They are of no use to him. Also they will help me to locate your position when I steer you in on your bikes on your next visit.

'That's how you did it!' The Twins exclaimed. Your telekinesis worked through the bracelets!'

'Don't ask me to explain my magic.' Maeneid laughed. 'And in return I won't ask you to explain yours.'

'Goodbye,' the Twins said sadly, poised on the one bike and ready to ride back into their own world.

'Farewell,' a variety of valedictory words were forthcoming from their comrades and Gorran and his subjects as the mists closed around the Twins and the bridge of time and its fairy folk faded into the realm of fantasy.

The Twins found the other bike leaning by the old oak tree and set off back towards Merebrook Manor.

'Time for lunch,' Sophie sent.

'Or time for tea,' Laura returned.

'**More like time for bed**,' they both sent together, looking at their fairy bracelets.

☪

OTHER TITLES IN THE
TWINS OF NETHERTIME SERIES

- BOOK ONE: THE SACRED EYES OF TIME
- BOOK TWO: THE OBELISK OF TIME
- BOOK THREE: THE TWINS OF NETHERTIME
- KA KA RANISH AND THE TWINS OF NETHERTIME
- THE TWINS OF NETHERTIME AND THE GOLDEN GROTTO
- THE TWINS OF NETHERTIME AND THE SEVEN SEAS OF TIME

Available from **Nethertime.co.uk** and **BonkerBooks.com**

ABOUT THE AUTHOR

I have spent a lot of my life travelling and encountered some very strange events, which no doubt filter on down into my writing.

After leaving grammar school in England, I joined the merchant navy as a navigation cadet officer and sailed around the world, though my enthusiasm for painting was always with me and after two years I jumped ship and enrolled in Art College. One year later I won a scholarship to the Royal College of Art in London. After getting an honours degree, I taught and exhibited widely, and then worked for the University of Chicago.

This was a challenging job - working in Egypt, recording the scenes on the eroded walls of tombs and temples in and around the Valley of the Kings - and it was to prove a lasting influence on my painting, poetry and writing. For in riding around the remote villages of Upper Egypt on my bike, my imagination was fired, and from that well of creativity emerged the characters and landscapes of the SERIES OF NETHERTIME.

But during this period, the surreal was not just confined to my fantasy novels; for many are the stories I could tell about being arrested for spying, robbed by camel-riding bandits and swimming the Nile in order to escape a pack of rabid dogs. These tales are too numerous for the telling here of course (maybe in another book)

After Egypt I lived for five years in the U.S.A. and Mexico, painting, writing, travelling and exhibiting, and ever amazed by the variety of wonderful landscape.

After America I lived in Scotland for ten years where I had the privilege of having Her Majesty the Queen and Prince Philip attend my exhibition.

But *the* event that changed my life was the birth of my twin daughters, Sophie and Laura who inspired me to start writing full time and are the protagonists in my fantasy series THE TWINS OF TIME.

Richard Turneramon

Lightning Source UK Ltd.
Milton Keynes UK
UKOW041914070413

208828UK00001B/4/P